PRAISE FOR
A QUIET APOCALYPSE

★★★★★

"I love [Dave Jeffery's] storytelling. This is one I can recommend to all readers, not just horror fans."
- AstraDaemon (via Amazon)

★★★★★

"It's relatable and grounded in reality offering a bleak view into the human psyche and herd mentality."
– D.T. Griffith (via Amazon)

★★★★★

"This story is heartbreaking, breathtaking and wholly original! Movie please! Highly recommended!"
– Kimnappi (via Amazon)

★★★★★

"Dave Jeffery offers us an eerily prescient and beautifully-realised novella: action-packed and emotional without being preachy or insincere. This is bleak horror with a heart (who thought that was even possible?). Highly recommended."
– Lovecat Kelso (via Amazon)

DEMAIN PUBLISHING

Short Sharp Shocks!

Book 0: Dirty Paws - Dean M. Drinkel
Book 1: Patient K - Barbie Wilde
Book 2: The Stranger & The Ribbon – Tim Dry
Book 3: Asylum Of Shadows – Stephanie Ellis
Book 4: Monster Beach – Ritchie Valentine Smith
Book 5: Beasties & Other Stories – Martin Richmond
Book 6: Every Moon Atrocious – Emile-Louis Tomas Jouvet
Book 7: A Monster Met – Liz Tuckwell
Book 8: The Intruders & Other Stories – Jason D. Brawn
Book 9: The Other – David Youngquist
Book 10: Symphony Of Blood – Leah Crowley
Book 11: Shattered – Anthony Watson
Book 12: The Devil's Portion – Benedict J. Jones
Book 13: Cinders Of A Blind Man Who Could See – Kev Harrison
Book 14: Dulce Et Decorum Est – Dan Howarth
Book 15: Blood, Bears & Dolls – Allison Weir
Book 16: The Forest Is Hungry – Chris Stanley
Book 17: The Town That Feared Dusk – Calvin Demmer
Book 18: Night Of The Rider – Alyson Faye
Book 19: Isidora's Pawn – Erik Hofstatter
Book 20: Plain – D.T. Griffith
Book 21: Supermassive Black Mass – Matthew Davis
Book 22: Whispers Of The Sea (& Other Stories) – L. R. Bonehill
Book 23: Magic – Eric Nash
Book 24: The Plague – R.J. Meldrum
Book 25: Candy Corn – Kevin M. Folliard
Book 26: The Elixir – Lee Allen Howard

Book 27: Breaking The Habit – Yolanda Sfetsos
Book 28: Forfeit Tissue – C. C. Adams
Book 29: Crown Of Thorns – Trevor Kennedy
Book 30: The Encampment / Blood Memory – Zachary Ashford
Book 31: Dreams Of Lake Drukka / Exhumation – Mike Thorn
Book 32: Apples / Snail Trails – Russell Smeaton
Book 33: An Invitation To Darkness – Hailey Piper
Book 34: The Necessary Evils & Sick Girl – Dan Weatherer
Book 35: The Couvade – Joanna Koch
Book 36: The Camp Creeper & Other Stories – Dave Jeffery
Book 37: Flaying Sins – Ian Woodhead
Book 38: Hearts & Bones – Theresa Derwin
Book 39: The Unbeliever & The Intruder – Morgan K. Tanner
Book 40: The Coffin Walk – Richard Farren Barber
Book 41: The Straitjacket In The Woods – Kitty R. Kane
Book 42: Heart Of Stone – M. Brandon Robbins
Book 43: Bits – R.A. Busby
Book 44: Last Meal In Osaka & Other Stories – Gary Buller
Book 45: The One That Knows No Fear – Steve Stred
Book 46: The Birthday Girl & Other Stories – Christopher Beck
Book 47: Crowded House & Other Stories - S.J. Budd
Book 48: Hand To Mouth – Deborah Sheldon
Book 49: Moonlight Gunshot Mallet Flame / A Little Death – Alicia Hilton
Book 50: Dark Corners - David Charlesworth

Murder! Mystery! Mayhem!

Maggie Of My Heart – Alyson Faye
The Funeral Birds – Paula R.C. Readman
Cursed – Paul M. Feeney

Beats! Ballads! Blank Verse!

Book 1: Echoes From An Expired Earth – Allen Ashley
Book 2: Grave Goods – Cardinal Cox
Book 3: From Long Ago – Paul Woodward
Book 4: Laws Of Discord – William Clunie

Anthologies

The Darkest Battlefield – Tales Of WW1/Horror

Horror Novellas

House Of Wrax – Raven Dane
A Quiet Apocalypse – Dave Jeffery

General Fiction

Joe – Terry Grimwood
Finding Jericho – Dave Jeffery

Science Fiction Collections

Vistas – Chris Kelso

Horror Fiction Collections

Distant Frequencies – Frank Duffy

A QUIET APOCALYPSE
BY DAVE JEFFERY

© Demain 2019

COPYRIGHT INFORMATION

Entire contents copyright © 2019 Dave Jeffery / Demain Publishing

Cover © 2019 Adrian Baldwin (www.adrianbaldwin.info)
Central cover image (C) 2019 Roberto Segate (https://www.roberto-segate.co.uk/)

First Published 2019

All rights reserved. No part of this publication may be reproduced, stored or transmitted in any form or by any means, electronic, mechanical, photocopying, recording, scanning or otherwise without written permission from the publisher. It is illegal to copy this book, post it to a website or distribute it by any other means without permission.

What follows is entirely a work of fiction. The names, characters and incidents portrayed in it are the work of the author's imagination. Any resemblance to actual persons, living or dead, events or localities is entirely co-incidental.

Dave Jeffery asserts the moral right to be identified as the author of this work in its totality.

Designations used by companies to distinguish their products are often claimed as trademarks. All brand names and product names used in this book and on its cover are trade names, service marks, trademarks and registered trademarks of their respective owners. The publishers and the book are not associated with any product or vendor mentioned in this book. None of the companies within the book have endorsed the book.

For further information, please visit:

WEB: www.demainpublishing.com
TWITTER: @DemainPubUk
FACEBOOK: Demain Publishing
INSTAGRAM: demainpublishing

Cover font: You Are Loved used under commercial license as granted to the designer by Kimberly Geswain. Read about Kimberly's work here: www.kimberlygeswein.com

CONTENTS

CHAPTER ONE	11
CHAPTER TWO	25
CHAPTER THREE	43
CHAPTER FOUR	51
CHAPTER FIVE	59
CHAPTER SIX	71
CHAPTER SEVEN	79
CHAPTER EIGHT	89
CHAPTER NINE	95
CHAPTER TEN	103
CHAPTER ELEVEN	123
CHAPTER TWELVE	131
CHAPTER THIRTEEN	137
CHAPTER FOURTEEN	148
CHAPTER FIFTEEN	155
CHAPTER SIXTEEN	165
CHAPTER SEVENTEEN	173
BIOGRAPHY	177
ADRIAN BALDWIN (COVER ARTIST)	178
DEMAIN PUBLISHING	181

*To the Deaf Communities of the world,
finding identity and strength in the silence.*

CHAPTER ONE

Someone once said that the world would end, not with a bang, but a whimper. Yet when the time came, the world could have died screaming until its lungs bled, and most would not have been able to hear anything at all.

That was the nature of the virus that silenced mankind.

The newscasts called the disease by its trade name, *bacterial meningitis*. But the scientists had defined it as MNG-U, or *Meningitis Unspecified*. I got to know this little nugget of wisdom later, after the disease had swept through my life, taking everything I held dear with it.

The symptoms began with pneumonia and rapidly accelerated to septicaemia as the blood became infected by streptococcus bacterium, inflaming the meninges in the brain and full-blown bacterial meningitis kicked in and turned the brain to steak-bake.

The angry storm left devastation in its wake. Those it didn't kill (and there weren't many it didn't) suffered gross brain damage and were left to die in hospitals that no longer had staff to treat them. Those who did survive the fevers came through the other side with profound deafness. The 'unspecified' element—the mutant strain—meant that symptoms of atypical meningitis could no longer be reversed.

MNG-U pitched up and decided to dig in and stay for a while. I have no idea how many died, I recall the reports on TV that said a third of the world population was *Triple-D* (dead, dying or deaf) before the medics knew what the hell was going on.

I do know that, of those rendered deaf, there are only a few hundred in the city we know as Cathedral. It is twenty miles south of here and fear and helplessness has made the population cruel, unsurprising as they are the remnants of an illness that was as wanton as it was deadly. Young, old, whatever in-between, it didn't have any preference who it affected, who it killed. It shared out the misery; the only true comfort came from ignorance and death.

After MNG-U moved on, a quiet apocalypse settled upon the landscape. The cries and shrieks may have faded for many, but for those very few of us who still retain our hearing, they are always there.

For they are our own.

***

A series of dull thuds break into the dream. It is a good dream—more memory than fantasy—and in the dream the world has not ended or been dragged back to an age where reason and civility are no longer constructs held in esteem. Instead there is the joy of loving someone, the warmth of an embrace, diversity and equity as much the essence of life as air itself.

The thuds are becoming insistent and I turn towards the sound with a groan. I don't need to open my eyes to distinguish who or what is trying to gain my attention. It is Crowley, my dependent, and he is using the large wooden stave he carries with him to beat a tattoo against my door frame. I also know if I do not rouse soon, he will come into the room and use it to give me extra incentive.

I sit up, the coarse material of my bedsheets itchy against the skin of my bare legs. As I turn to face Crowley, he stops attacking the wooden jamb and stands staring at me, his eyes alert and the *Tell-Pad* is insistent.

GET UP – NOW!

I grab the case containing a small keyboard on my bedside table. There is an LED screen embedded in the outside of the lid so when open Crowley can see what I type scrolling across the screen.

WHAT IS IT?

DUSTCLOWD. ON TTHE ROAD. FUCKIN SAMARITANZ.

YOU SURE?

YES. GETT THE FUK UP!

When I climb from my bed, I am cautious not to let my bare feet linger too long on the threadbare, tacky rug. I gingerly stretch my right leg, feel the grimace setting up camp on my face as the limb protests at the movement I try to instil. It's not been the same since Crowley went to work on the kneecap with a hammer over a year ago, my penance for trying to escape. Now I cannot stand without the makeshift brace I have to wear, Crowley's Gift to make sure I can still serve his needs.

He's all heart.

After getting my leg to behave I put on my trousers and fumble with the boots. I stand, placing all my weight on my left foot, and then I reach for Crowley's Gift. It is a contraption made up of steel strips, articulated at the knee with loose bolts, and secured to my leg with leather straps. When it's not in use, propped up against the wall next to my bed, it looks like a piece of deranged Meccano. Without it, I must drag my leg like the heavy, useless lump of meat it has become. Sometimes I need Crowley to help me, co-dependents in misery.

Still, it's the least he can fucking do.

***

Sometimes I struggle to remember what it is like to have hope. These days it's an elusive entity, like a day free from Crowley's scowl. The weather doesn't help. Thunderheads wheel in from the west, bringing with them dreary light as fat raindrops fall, hitting my poncho like the bodies of dead birds splattering the asphalt. Beneath my poncho, my arms are in sleeves that are stitched to a belt harness giving my limbs limited movement.

I lean forward, giving my hands a chance to pull my baseball cap down to protect my face from the rain. A trickle of water exploits a small gap in the collar of the poncho and begins a slow, icy descent, causing an involuntary shudder. I shuffle on the camping chair, rubbing my back in the upright until the raindrop is wiped dry against my shirt, though my eyes remain fixed on the road running past the village, making sure it is clear, safe. I chew on my gum shield, the thick plastic sticking to my mouth. To keep it in place, a leather thong wraps about my mouth and cheeks. I have to breathe through my nose or the gaps left available to my lips.

Crowley is beside me, sat in his own chair, wearing his own poncho, holding the leash of twine and strips of leather, braided and tethering us together. He, too, is scanning the featureless countryside, yet I know it is fear that keeps him alert, fear of losing me to the Samaritans.

We see them on the edge of the field, where the road creates a grey scar in the landscape. The men and women are turned to mere shadows by the distance, the long trench coats flap wildly as they pile out of the back of a brown, flatbed truck.

Each has a slab of white light on their chest, hanging from a bulky chain about their necks. There is also a domed shoulder lamp, a coiled wire trailing into a fat black fuse box on each belt. The lamp occasionally blinks yellow like a car indicator, alerting the owner that one of their group is communicating with them.

There is a dog with them, an Alsatian, and it lurches forward, making its leash taut until its handler yanks it to heel. Apparently, we're lucky the Samaritans don't have bloodhounds. Crowley tells me if that was the case, the scent traps we use would be useless as those animals are the Ferrari of search dogs. I don't consider myself lucky, not now. My luck ran out when my beautiful family were taken by the fever.

The dog makes no sound; it—too—has lost something. The vocal cords would have been cut as a pup, no good hunting the hearing with a barking mutt giving the game away.

Games. It's all games these days, Hide and Seek, Cat and Mouse.

Hangman.

The trees outside the cities are adorned with the bodies of usurpers, those who simply cannot fit in with the new world order. Instead, they swing on the breeze, faces bloated and black, gravity working its science as flesh and cloth become indistinguishable from each other, ghoulish baubles of barbarism, the juices of decay falling to the ground, absorbed by the earth, the corruption spreading out across the land until nothing is left untainted, and innocence is a sullied entity screaming and alone in the cold, cold darkness.

I suck in air and close off errant thoughts of death and helplessness. There is never a good time to revisit great loss, especially when it's still as raw as a skinned knee.

The adage 'time heals' is a lie.

Over time the Samaritans have evolved from a rag-tag shit-show to an efficient machine with the sole purpose of neutering autonomy and perpetuating the commodity of hearing to those who cannot. They move in groups of three—one driver, two trackers. All carry sidearms and tasers of bright yellow. I know this as I have seen them up close and personal. They are indefatigable in their purpose, relentless in their duty.

They roam the plains looking for people like me. People who can still hear. When they find The Hearing, they take us away to the city known as Cathedral. What they do with us there is a mystery to everyone. Only the Samaritans know the fate of those they take. Yet I know why they would drag me away from Crowley.

It is about control.

Communication is now commodity. In those of us who can still hear, the Samaritans see the path to power. Safety and security have now become as much a utility as water and electricity. Such things are still available, Cathedral is functioning, but any sense of society is small scale, generators and dried produce creating market districts, governed by some overlord or other. Food, water and the comfort of light and heat are paltry compared to living in a world of silence. I know this because Crowley tells me about what it is like to be deaf.

Through his own *Tell-Pad* he articulates about the isolation, the sense of perpetual fear of not being able to know if someone, something, is creeping up on you, imparting all of this on a small keypad he keeps in his pocket. He tells his story on the seven-inch screen secured to his broad chest by a harness of thin leather belts. This yoke of anguish often comes alive with misspelt words and grammatically fucked up sentences creating an image of bitterness and despair.

I am immune to his rhetoric; he is disabled whereas I am a slave. I have no more sympathy for him as I would the animals we hunt and eat to continue to live in this God forsaken wilderness. Every evening I must sit and watch his rambling, self-pitying script from the confines of my 'quarters', the prison cell with soft furnishing. I'm not sure if he sees me as boon or curse, a thing that he cannot be without yet a constant reminder of what he has lost.

But he is not prepared to lose me.

The arm restraints, leash and gum-shield are compulsory when I am outside. They are symbols of slavery in this world of silence.

And such is Crowley's paranoia; he thinks I'd rather jump from the frying pan of a life with him into the hellfire of Cathedral. No chances are ever taken when Samaritans are near, no corners cut in Crowley's bid to keep his prize.

As I watch the scent-hound cock its leg and piss on the rear wheel of the flatbed, I wonder if Crowley sees me as nothing more than an expedient beast.

Across the valley the truck fires up its engine and doors thud shut after securing the dog in the trailer. The vehicle reverses, and then pulls an arc to face the direction of Cathedral.

With a roar and a fart of diesel smoke, it drives away and, for the first time in an hour, I feel the leash about my neck go slack.

***

In the kitchen we sit at a wooden farmhouse table. Overhead, the lights embedded in the ceiling are low, the dimmer switch set to its nadir and the curtains—double lined to make sure not even the meagre light can ooze through the material—are drawn tight. The whole room has a conspiratorial air about it as we sit hunched over plates of tinned ham and boiled potatoes.

Beside my plate is my *Tell-Pad*, open and ready to engage if needed.

As is his way, Crowley's eyes never leave me as he chews his food. They scrutinise like a hawk seeking out prey on the landscape below, their slate-grey irises cold and steeped in suspicion and paranoia. It is as though he waits for the muscles of my face to betray any thoughts of rebellion and deception. On occasion his stare is so intense, his eyes so unfathomable, that I expect him to one day launch across the table and put his steak knife through my neck and watch me bleed out onto the Wedgewood dinner service and condiments. I look down at my plastic knife and fork and wonder when things became so one-sided.

Crowley is particularly tense tonight; I know this by the way his fists clench around the cutlery and it remains hard to clear my mind of the image of an imminent assault. I suspect it is due to the Samaritans being so close to the boundary.

They've been here before, of course, back in the early days when the search for hearing people had a desperate, disorganised flavour to it, the kind of flavour that left a bad taste and bodies on the ground. In these times, Crowley had dragged me to a wood store beyond the tree line. I was left there for a small lifetime, without food or water, until he returned in the fading daylight. In my panic to be free of that accursed place I'd knocked him aside, earning me a whack to the head from the butt of his rifle. The blow put me out for a few hours and when I came to I found him watching me with the same expression he now wears across the table.

I watch his *Tell-Pad* spark to life. He has set an alert tone to make sure I have his undivided attention. An electronic bell sounds like its calling one of Pavlov's dogs. My eyes flit to the screen.

I SEE YOU.

I shrug my shoulders; his comment makes no sense.

YOUR UP 2 SOMTHIN. ITS IN YOUR EYZ.

My shaking head doesn't appear to be tempering his paranoia. Seems the Samaritans' visit has perhaps shaken him more than usual. I suspect he's become an addict of sorts; dependent on the connection I give him to the world that is lost to him. And like an addict, he loves and hates what holds him to ransom, but he cannot bear the thought of misplacing his fix. I must be cautious; Crowley is a man of impulse. The last time I failed to realise this nuance, it cost me a kneecap.

JUST THINKING ABOUT THOSE SAMARITANS.

Crowley's eyes narrow, his eyebrows form a valley of grey thicket.

WHAT ABOUT EM?

THEY WERE CLOSER TO THE BOUNDARY THAN USUAL. MAYBE WE NEED TO RESET THE SCENT TRAP?

Crowley thinks this through before hitting the keyboard. He is nodding as he types.

OK. DAWN TOMOROW. GETT TO BED.

I sit back in my chair, trying not to let my face give away the irritation in my chest at being sent to my room like an ill-disciplined five-year-old. I console myself as I stand and turn away from him, heading to my room while singing 'mother-fucker' over and over to the tune of Old MacDonald Had a Farm.

CHAPTER TWO

In my room I fuel the petulant child analogy by sulking on my bed. The mattress is lumpy, the duvet so old the duck and down feathers pierce the material in places, jabbing at the exposed skin of my arms as I lie back to stare at the undulating ceiling made of beam and thick plaster.

At least winter is still a few months away. Crowley allows an oil burner in my room during the colder months, and then only if the temperatures fall below zero. I have spent three seasons on the farm and know how cold it gets within the stone walls of this prison masquerading as a home.

The room is large, the floors uneven and covered, for the most part, by that hideous rug of gaudy reds and purples. It's hard not to wish it was a flying carpet that would give me the means to escape. Instead it is a threadbare, dusty relic from a time for which I have neither knowledge nor interest. This is a piece of Crowley's history, not mine. The thought of how I got to be here seeps into my consciousness, and I shove it back into the darkness like a dirty compromise. Like an oiled snake the memories slither free and present like a crazed orator at Speaker's Corner, demanding to be heard.

Images of a pitiable exodus of one as I leave my dead, desolate village weeks after the last emergency broadcasts disappear from the TV screens.

Watching the horizon turn to smoke and flame as things get ugly in the larger towns and cities. Alone and grieving, for me, my family, humanity, stumbling through roads littered with the material trappings of 21st Century life and the horrors of the new order.

The people I meet are few and far between, but I find a hearing survivor, a middle-aged lady called Rose who used to be a bank manager. She tells me of what is happening in the city of Cathedral, and I cannot quite believe it. The next day Rose is caught by what I now know are Samaritans and she is shown as an example of their absolute purpose; dragged away screaming out my name as I hide like a weasel in the undergrowth.

I avoid Samaritans after I witness their deeds and intentions. Their barbarism forces me away from the streets and into the fields. Then my greatest mistake to date: hiding out and falling asleep in one of

Crowley's barns, and waking up with him standing over me.

The rest, as it goes, is history.

This story comes to mind often, along with many others that bring with them anguish. I wish I didn't cling to them so and I wonder if, sometimes, I need them in order to find some good in my current dilemma.

Across the room is a dressing table of deep brown wood. It has an arched mirror that casts my pathetic reflection, head propped on two shapeless pillows, face sallow even under the muted light from the bedside table lamp. My tall, gangly frame lies ungainly on the mattress, like a crane fly that's made a particularly poor landing. I used to take pride in my appearance. Pride and appearance were virtues of my father.

Daddy Dearest also worked miracles. For over ten years he was able to live two lives. The first as a caring, sharing dad and husband, the second as boyfriend to someone I never got to meet, but my mother christened, "That bitch".

I wonder what life would have been like if my mother hadn't found the second cell phone down the back of the sofa; if she hadn't sparked it up and seen the messages on the home screen. Words of love and lust creating an introduction to betrayal. My father left home on my tenth birthday. The memory of the night he did an about-face and marched out of my life forever tarnished my thinking for many years.

The fallout still resonates, the crying and screaming; the inevitable apologies and regrets, the latter more a lament to losing the phone in the first place, I suspect. The conceit had mileage, putting dear Dad on a road to complacency city.

He paid the price, kicked out of the family home, sent packing from his long-standing lover's place too when she found out he'd no intention of divorcing my mother without a fight. Not even his excuse that it was down to getting his share of the finances could save him. "That bitch" wanted *him*, not the cash, it seemed, and she too became collateral damage in this war of betrayal. But she came out fighting and retreated after inflicting as much emotional damage upon my father as she could.

The divorce was brutal and bitter and left my mother broken for a while. Antidepressants and psychological therapy bolstered and eventually rebuilt her battered self-esteem. But she contributed to the bruise on my ego that would yellow but never fade.

Rejection is a parasite that has fed off my psyche for as long as I can remember, though I have often sought to deny its existence. Mother became an actress in the time that followed; the persona one of resolution and stoicism, each nuance layered to dampen down her devastation at a life gone awry.

My grandparents took us in, and for months afterwards I acquired the ability to stop conversations dead whenever I walked into a room. So, I stopped going into the rooms, choosing instead to sidle up outside, listening to adult conversations with young ears, trying to make sense of words such as 'affair' and 'divorce' and 'whoring bastard'.

And then there were the nights I heard my mother crying softly through the thin plaster wall separating our bedrooms. But it was to be emotional barriers that laid the foundations for estrangement.

The very first night my mother's muted weeping came to me, I climbed from my bed, bare feet crossing naked boards, and snuck out of my bedroom. I found my mother shuddering beneath a mound of blankets, an empty bottle of scotch on the bedside table. The door drifted open, the hallway light throwing a creamy rectangle upon the floor, my silhouette small and dark—a literal shadow of my former self. From the bed, my mother had groaned a protest at being disturbed, this rising to a short, sharp yell as I'd asked her if she was okay.

That day, the feeling my mother's rebuke put in my heart is her legacy, a brand that, until I met Evie, my future wife, stalled my ability to form lasting relationships with women. Emotions were a bright fusion of anger and jealousy, constant fear of being rejected. So, I'd do what seemed right, I'd regain control of tail-spinning emotions by ending the affairs, usually in a drink-fuelled rage.

Some would consider the fractured family a cliché-riddled origin for rejection. I say it is usually those who have no concept of growing up with instability, uncertainty and the fear that the only parent who is left doesn't want you either. For a long time, I held such people in contempt but as Evie worked her magic, I came to understand it was ignorance and convenience that drove the mindsets of naysayers.

I am a truism—the proverbial cliché—and I'm not embarrassed but comforted by this truth. I am a product of my life, and the terrible things that are in it. And there have been only bad things to draw upon until now, the loss of my family, the loss of civilisation and the heinous caricature that serves as its replacement.

At the time the fever made its way through our lives, my mother had remarried a sensible, reliable man called Tony and moved down on the coast. Evie and I would go and see her and Tony every few months. Last thing I heard about Dad was that he'd shacked up with a 24-year-old and her toddler. There were rumours he was also seeing another girl who looked ridiculously like my mother. History repeats like a bad meal.

But in the end, nothing really matters, those who gave me love, those I loved, are as dead as those who did nothing to offer me such things, nor I in return.

Good, bad or indifferent mean nothing to disease.

***

Crowley has me walking the boundary line. The grass is wet with morning dew, the dawn light, muted. The Samaritans will not venture out after dusk or before the sun is well up in the sky. Even with their guns and tasers and dogs.

They know their vulnerabilities all too well; it is these very same foibles that make people such as me so valuable. The absence of Samaritans means that I am also free of my weatherproof strait-jacket, leash and mouthguard.

I take in the dawn air; the smell of the wet grass is sweet and clears away heavy thoughts. I love being outside. It would be even better if I was not about to stink up the place with the piece of cod that has been put into a plastic freezer-bag and left outside overnight.

My thoughts slow my pace which earns me an impatient snort from Crowley. He stands several feet away, well inside the boundary, and his rifle is steadfast in his hands, the barrel aimed at my legs in case I can somehow get my malformed knee to function again and go sprinting off across the fields like Usain fucking Bolt.

The scent trap has a complex process, but the purpose is rudimentary; we use it to become invisible to the world about us, especially the Samaritans and their dogs. If the hounds smell the fish first and not the man, then we are invisible, Crowley has assured me. I'm not sure I understand one hundred percent how this procedure works but it involves the dog finding the fish scent a more powerful lure, so strong in fact, it does not have to use the ground where it's more likely to pick up more interests, in particular the tell-tale signs of the men trying to dupe it.

This works, of course, because the Samaritans have the dogs going in nose blind. With no original trail to follow our hunters must literally stumble across our scent, and the fish I will pull along the boundary with transparent line is the means by which we remain aurally incognito. The hypoallergenic gloves I wear will make sure our ruse is not usurped at the last moment.

I pull the line from my pockets and prepare the fishhook. Carefully I draw the plastic zipper on the freezer bag, my nose wrinkling and the stink that is released. Ramming the hook into the cod steak, I test it is secure before dropping it to the long grass. Then I proceed to walk slowly, the dew making my trousers wet and putting a shine on my wellington boots. After three hundred yards, I stop near the great oak that is destined to become complicit in our ruse.

Detaching the line from the puckered fillet, I take aim and launch the fish skywards, where it arcs and lands high in the branches of the tree. The job done, I can now retrace my steps, my presence now a ghost in the Piscean scent left for the dogs that will follow, if not today, then in some near future.

It is as I wind in the line, eyes cast down to the grass, that I see the silver-grey figure of eight lying in the grass. When I see the speaker grille and the tuning dials, I hold my breath and look up to find Crowley. He remains distant but I know he literally has me in his sights, a bullet in the breech ready for any of my 'funny business'.

I coil the line, securing it with a slipknot. Keeping it casual, I drop the coiled line, stooping immediately to catch it. As my hand snags the nylon, so too does it snake into the long grass to grab the object. In one swift movement both are scooped up and shoved deep into the thigh pockets of my cargo pants as I stand upright.

A pounding heart keeps my company on the walk back to Crowley, anxiety and excitement fuelling this engine of tissue and muscle. But it is not the visceral that keeps me going, it is something quite different that makes me feel lightheaded. At this moment my heart contains so much more than valve, aorta and blood. It is made light by hope.

As I approach Crowley, a blade of ice cuts through my sternum as I look at the TP on his chest and his hand reaches out, his open palm, pale and expectant.

The words on the screen are like a scream that is so loud it stops time.

HAND IT OVR. NOW!

Although my lungs are curtains of steel and my breath stutters in my chest, I act casual. I shrug, freezing my shoulders at mid-point, holding out my hands, palms turned to the pale sky, the universal stance of the innocent.

"What?" I mouth the word, exaggerating the expression. Crowley hates me doing this as it makes him feel stupid. He told me this the first time I did it, following the confession with a punch to the face. It took my cheek a week to deflate, two for the yellow-purple bruises beneath my left eye to fade.

But Crowley doesn't take the bait, instead he hits his TP keyboard taped to his free arm.

NO BULLSHITT. HAND OVR THE LINE.

I swallow a cry of relief. The line, he wants the coil of fishing line and hook I used as a lure for the scent trap! I dig into my pocket after a pause, my fingertips touching the cold plastic of the radio. A thrill passes through me as though my fingers trace across the skin of a wanton lover.

I pull the coil free and hold it out towards Crowley. He snatches it from me and stuffs it into the breast pocket of his body warmer. He activates the TP soon after.

GET BACK TO HOWSE.

I think of the radio and its opportunities before heading back across the fields, Crowley and his rifle at my back. I carry my own means of protection, the smile that my master cannot see is as powerful as any fist or boot or rifle.

***

It is later; the day feels stretched, as though time has become fudge left out in the midday sun. The thought of the radio is the catalyst, of course. For hours I have longed to get into my room and explore the plastic carcass. Keeping patience has been almost as tough as keeping up appearances so that Crowley does not suspect things are amiss, that things are *different*.

I go through the motions: running maintenance on the generators, chopping wood for the burner with a small, pathetic hatchet and at gunpoint to make sure there is no sudden rebellion. Daily chores, each one a countdown of the day, and all the time my heart quickening with excitement and fear. Excitement, because there is a chance to at least connect with the outside world, and fear based on the very real possibility that the radio was discarded because it is useless.

At eight in the evening Crowley goes to his drinks cabinet and pulls out his bottle of hooch. He distils the shit from potato peelings and when he spills any of it on the kitchen floor, the clear liquid leaves clear spots like bleach on coloured linen. In a few hours, I'll no doubt hear his coughing fits through the floor of my room. I'm hoping the damn stuff is killing him from the inside, but the bastard seems to have the constitution of a lead-lined bucket. As the glass and bottle hit the table, it's my cue to retire to my cell with its shitty rug and corrugated furniture.

The ritual begins. I get up, Crowley follows on behind as we navigate the full, bleak corridors leading to the stairway. I mount the stairs, the motion orchestrated by the creak of risers and the ratcheted squeaks of Crowley's Gift.

I open the door to my room on the first landing and I know that as I enter, Crowley watches, his hand placed flat against the wall of the stair well. He will not come up here until I am safe inside, and the door shut tight, the self-locking mechanism installed just for my benefit. He will follow once his hand on the wall feels the vibration of the door slamming shut.

Yes, he will lumber upstairs, and I will hear him test that the heavy oak is stout in its frame, hear him pause for breath as though going through the motions of listening out for mischief. Sometimes, I swear I can hear him sniffing and snorting like a foraging hog before he tramps back down to his kitchen, to his bottle of carefree oblivion.

***

Like Crowley's bottle of hooch, we all have our vices, and mine now rests on my lap. I sit on the bed and peer down at the radio as though for the first time. The device is small, fashioned from tough, weatherproof plastic and is shaped as a figure of eight. The radio is well-worn; there are tiny scratches on the casing. The crank-handle is an inner circle of tough black plastic in the upper half of the figure-eight. It pulls forward on a centralised hinge that also doubles as the gyro-motor once the crank engages at forty-five degrees.

Again, the handle is scuffed with use and I imagine the device sitting in a camp, a family huddled about a fire as the weekend in the wild draws them all together after a week spent bringing home the bacon. The image is so vivid I feel the corners of my mouth tugging into a smile that stays for a few seconds, a potent reminder of the power of a warm thought or good memory. The smile falters, the cold winds of reality leave their chill in my heart and thoughts turn back to the device in my palm.

I slowly turn the crank. There is token resistance as the gears inside the gyro engage and a metallic wheeze announces the mechanism is alive and well. Relief leaves my shoulders light and my heart fluttering with excitement. I turn the crank through its cycle for a second time, and then a third, and a fourth, continuing until the gyro lets me know it is maxed out by locking the gears.

I fold the crank back into its housing and turn the radio over so that I can see the facia. There is a single tuning dial and a horizontal bandwidth bar. To my delight, a small LED light tells me two things. The first is that somehow, this device is working as it should. The second is that perhaps, just this once, luck has somehow reached into the darkness and grabbed my shivering, outstretched hands.

Without warning the device comes alive, the crackle and hiss abrupt. Instinctively my fingers scramble for the volume control, a shudder of fear passing through me. Then I remember the condition of my gaoler and relax, calming my breathing until my heart returns to its customary pace.

Listening to the sizzle and pop, I pinch the tuning dial and carefully turn, as my labours are acknowledged by the undulating tone coming through the grille.

My eyes watch the orange thread stroll across the frequency window until there is no more place to go. I feel a little deflated but temper this with rational thinking. There might not be anything transmitting now, but at another time on another day, something may well emerge through the static fog.

This thought gives me peace for the evening. I use the time to carefully find a spot to stash my newfound sense of freedom. Under the mattress seems the obvious place, but I know Crowley sees this room as it is, a prison that robs me of opportunity and any chance of conceit.

His ignorance is also a weapon and I shall use it to my advantage. Besides, there is a comfort going to sleep knowing you are lying in a bed now dedicated to clandestine freedom.

CHAPTER THREE

I have been holding my late-night vigils with the radio for well over a week, and my frustration is starting to build. All that greets my efforts are the unwavering hisses, no matter how slowly I turn the dial. I hate the fact that I am becoming despondent. The sensation is all too familiar as it suckles on my fledgling optimism, draining it away until I am dangerously close to becoming disillusioned.

This is the climate in which I have decided to take a risk. I must attempt to try accessing the frequency ranges during the daylight hours. As much as I'd like to try the radio outside of this room, I cannot take the chance of being found and have Crowley confiscate and ultimately smash the thing—and my fortunes—into pieces. So, I'm now getting up earlier, while Crowley snores down the hallway. Despite the hooch and no further need for a call to market, he's still a farmer so rises slightly too early for my tastes. It all feels like it is part of the conspiracy that thwarts my opportunity of being alone with the device on which I have pinned so much.

Of course, the fleeting thought that I may have placed too much faith in this saviour drops in occasionally. But I can quash it for the time being. I must, there's simply too much to lose.

I'm on the edge of my bed, leaning forwards as though immersed in a great novel, the kind that has the gift of taking you away from the places causing ill. The radio continues with its familiar, never ending static and I hear the heavy thump and creak of floorboards as Crowley climbs from his bed.

I fumble with the dial, searching for the off switch when the room is suddenly filled with the warm sound of a voice uttering eight wonderful words.

"If you can hear me, dear traveller, rejoice!"

I almost cry out with happiness, but this is quickly tempered as I hear Crowley going through his ablutions in his room. It is only a matter of time before he will be at my door with his surly manner and his demands.

I note the frequency window—98 megahertz—and turn off the radio, storing it back under my mattress. The elation is incredible, reminding me of the time Evie said she would accept my marriage proposal, or when she'd told me she was pregnant, and later that year when I witnessed Poppy's birth. All these things smashing together and almost taking my breath away.

The decision to engineer a way to spend more time with the radio during daylight hours comes swiftly, the means by which I could achieve it is not very well thought through.

Crowley's boots are thumping across the landing and approaching the door, the rattle of keys muted beyond by the heavy oakwood. I scuttle over to the dressing table and take a breath.

My target is the edge of the dresser, my weapon is my forehead. I drop my bodyweight as I bend in the middle, the dresser rushing up towards me.

I figure it's effective because the next thing I see is Crowley leaning over me with a bag of ice. When the makeshift compress connects with my aching forehead, my vision swims and I feel like throwing up.

Yet it all feels worthwhile when sabotage works in your favour.

***

Crowley's haggard, wizened face looms over me, his countenance surly as he puts the makeshift ice pack on my brow, and I flinch at both the sensation of cold and hot pain that shoots through my head. Eyes closed, I groan, and my grumpy nursemaid thumps the mattress to get my attention. I squint, my vision wavering, the *Tell-Pad* is inches from my face, the screen shimmies as I try to focus.

WHAT FUK HAPEND?

He shoves the keyboard in my hands, and I try to protest as bright sparkles join my oscillating vision. Pained, I respond.

HITT MMY HED

FUNNY. HOW???

HAV A GESS.

For a short time, Crowley's face is bemused then his eyes drop to my leg. His shoulders sag as he buys the story. My brain may be temporarily scrambled, but I can still tell a tale. I wonder in this moment if Crowley feels guilt for what he has done.

STAY HEAR. BASTRD.

I guess not.

Eyes now closed, I feel the bed bounce as the mattress is relieved of his weight. This is followed by heavy footfalls as he moves away. The door finally closes with a familiar thud. In harmony with the door, my mind decides to shut down for a while.

When I wake the headache is bearable. I open my eyes and the light is muted to the point where I feel I have been out for most of the day, and panic that my self-induced head trauma has been for nothing. Instead, I see the blinds are now drawn and there is a plate of chunky sandwiches and a water pitcher on my side table. The door across the room is closed once more and the house is silent. I assume Crowley has started the daily routine, leaving me to rest.

I catch my reflection in the dressing table and, despite the dark egg in the centre of forehead making me look like some half-arsed cyclops, I am smiling.

The seeds I have sown are now ready for reaping. As I reach for the radio from beneath the mattress, I begin to pray to a God I don't believe exists that the harvest is plentiful.

***

For once a plan comes to fruition. It is a mere ten minutes and the voice returns, sending a lightning-strike of pure joy through my body.

The woman on the radio speaks and I listen, mesmerised like a 3rd grader on the story time mat. As her voice oozes from the device, I stare at the grille as though my willpower would suddenly have her appear.

"Castles have dungeons," she says. "But dungeons still have doors, and doors are either a way to keep you in, or the way to break out."

It's fustian, but I go with it, swept along with the moment. Captivated by the optimism.

The promise.

"Be free of your prison. You should not be punished for being able to hear. Come, traveller, find us, here at *The Refuge*. This is your place, a utopia, free from emancipation, free from tyranny."

Buying into the patter is easy; the woman's voice is like silk, the intonation: cream over ice. I'm a consumer lapping up the pitch and reaching for my wallet.

The pitch of the voice coming over long-silent airwaves reminds me of Evie. As always memories arrive with a layer of shit that I must clear away to get to the fertile, well-nourished soil.

Evie's face comes to me and it is as it was in her final moments on the Earth, screaming as the fever baked her brain until blood came from her eyes. The image of red tears streaming down her alabaster cheeks is one that is always ripe and ready to return.

I lose myself in the sultry speech oozing from the radio and in my mind the voice morphs into that of my wife and I think of her as a thing of great beauty, her lithe frame, thighs toned from her early morning runs, the smile that slips across her face as my hand takes a stroll across her small breast, fingertips doing a pirouette on her pink nipples.

The image is vivid—hypnotic—and its grip over me is assured, my hands take hold of myself and engage in the escalating rhythm until the deed is done, and I press a forearm into my mouth as ecstasy claims me, and weep, the meat of my arm stifling sobs that no-one is destined to hear.

CHAPTER FOUR

The radio is to become my solace in this world of silent slavery. If he finds out, I know Crowley will smash it and beat me, and not necessarily in that order.

It will be fear that drives him, fear of being cut off from the sounds that emerge from the vertical grille of the black speakers, the words that he would never be able to hear, never be able to vet.

And not just the rhetoric that comes with the words and sounds, but their meaning—their influence—on his hearing servant. Without me he is alone, his vulnerabilities exposed to the hazards that roam the blighted landscapes beyond his land.

The dangers out there are very real, I can hear things in the night, even from the confines of my cell. Animals baying and growling, the rumble of distant vehicles as they pass by, the sound of fat, greasy engines carried for miles on the empty air.

And as these sounds come to me, I picture who or what could be making them, though I already have a pretty good idea.

But all these thoughts are not redundant or futile; instead they help pass the time as I wait for The Voice. When it comes through the grille I am filled with both awe and anxiety.

These emotions always come in close succession as she continues her spiel. The pace is sedate, almost pedestrian, as though she is carefree in this debilitated world. I imagine her sitting back on a barstool, glass of chilled Sauvignon Blanc in her hand, a giggle at the back of her throat. Wherever she is, I know that she feels safe enough to take her time, her oratory sliding through to the listener with the ease of a cold beer down the gullet on a hot summer's day.

When I first heard the message, I thought it may have been a recording, the voice of someone long since dead. But the words seem current, the flavour of the narrative reflective of the season, or the weather, and the time of day. The woman is very much here and now, and the thought of being able to go and find the place—The Refuge—promising halcyon days, gives me excitement not felt for such a long time, it breaks through the weariness and the omnipotent horror that have been my bedfellows for what seems like eons.

I get up and stroll to the window. The view is limited by the woodlands; the crowded trees a swaying, green entity that broils like a Sargasso Sea. In Spring the breeze brings with it the smell of honeysuckle and cherry blossom. In Winter, the fragrant aroma of woodland primrose. These come to me through the small gap the retainer secured to the window frame allows. Then, of course, there are the bars, screwed to the outside wall, and making sure I stay-put.

I am a prisoner, sentenced to life without parole. The small things in life are now monumental. The smell through the window, the radio.

My reflections become an unstable scaffold upon which I lose my footing. I fall headlong into the depths of sleep, the debris of a past tumbling with me, as determined to claim me in slumber's deep embrace. In the netherworld of dream and reality, images play out, and I am their hapless, helpless witness.

***

We stand at the spot known as *Jean's Place*, the cairn rising from the lush, wet grass like a great, scaly slug crawling from the earth. It is September 13th, the birthday of Crowley's dear departed wife. This is a ritual, a memorial to a woman I've never met. For all I know, Jean could have been a kind soul, with a big heart. She may have sat in the kitchen, nursing a pot of tea, brewed strong and sweet, fresh bread and jam on thick plates laid out on the workhorse of a table. There may have been kids in the house at some point, maybe they'd grown up and left home.

More likely Jean was a bitch with a bastard husband and their offspring now dead.

Crowley is now standing beside me, his head bowed as the sunlight plays in the boughs overhead. The shadows from the branches cast oscillating shapes on the grave as though flat, black fingers writhe over the stones, the Hand of Death still determined to make His presence known.

But the Reaper has never really left these lands. On some days, when the winds come in from the north-west, it brings the sweet purulent stink of decay; from the meadows and the valleys, the villages and hamlets. It is the scent of loss, the cologne of chaos, making known—just in case we can ever forget—the true fate of mankind.

Crowley hangs his head as though in shame, though I doubt he has concept of such an ethic. The construct of morality is as fluid today as it has ever been. Social tenets and existential crises are the new gods in this imbalanced world of haves and have-nots. It is as though the struggles of the twenty-first century have ballooned into a bloated parody of importance. Gone are notions of rights, there is only the need to feel safe no matter what the cost to those poor souls forced to provide it.

As Crowley nurtures his grief, so it is that I turn to notions of hope in the form of my radio, and the mesmerising words from my saviour on the airwaves. Just as birdsong from the woodlands crosses the valley, so too does her sweet voice, seducing with words of possible futures.

My tranquil thoughts are interrupted by Crowley. His thick voice comes to me, a dirty rock hitting the still waters of the crystal-clear lake that is my reverie.

I look over to him, surprised that he is not focused on me at all, his eyes are closed, and he is taking in air through his nostrils. He reminds me of Jerry the mouse sniffing the air when Tom the cat is about to eat a freshly cooked steak, stolen from the kitchen of his disembodied owner.

Abruptly, Crowley turns and extends an arm before stabbing a finger towards a section of trees. I recognise the spot; it is a path leading to a copse deep in the heart of the woods. As I turn to face the trees, I realise what has Crowley so badly riled.

I smell smoke and the sweet, sweet smell of fried bacon. But it also indicates

Crowley has a trespasser with a campfire and griddle. I know what is coming next, even before I look into Crowley's haunted eyes.

***

Crowley is so twitched I have been entrusted with the baton. I figure that he is prepared to take the risk since he has retrieved his rifle from the farmhouse before handing it to me. These days, the odds are forever in his favour.

But his concerns are equally as real to me. The campfire is giving off smoke and the delicious smells of a cooked breakfast. To the Samaritans and their hounds, we may as well send up a flare. The wood burner back at the farmhouse is never lit during the daylight hours for this very reason. There is a simple commonality uniting prisoner and guard, neither of us want the Samaritans anywhere near us.

So, I'm moving as fast as my crippled leg will allow. Crowley's Gift rattles and jitters as I navigate the undergrowth. I use a nearby oak tree for both support and cover. I am the clumsy chameleon, the inept interloper. But this is not an issue when it comes to the hunt.

Not anymore.

Ahead is my prey. A man sitting at a campfire, I hear the crackles and snaps as the flames eat away at the dry twigs, sending a lazy squall of grey smoke up into the woodland roof. He has his back to me, but I can see long tendrils of grey-black hair emerging from a beaten, brown fedora. These locks crawl down his denim shirt. He is lean and able, more than enough to cause me issue should he suspect my presence.

Not that he ever will, of course.

About him are the man's possessions, a discarded long coat and a rucksack is nearby. The pack is partially empty and sits wrinkled and squat like an old man's penis. On the other side of the man I see the rifle. The sight of it makes me pause, despite my ready advantage.

I know nothing about guns, makes and models, magazine capacity, and all the survivalist shit I used to see on the internet, means nothing. I only know what they are designed to do, and given this man is alone and out in the wilds says to me that he knows exactly what to do with it and does it well. Suddenly the baton in my hand feels inadequate, a reflection of me as a person since the world turned to shit.

I continue onwards, towards the unsuspecting figure as he messes with his campfire. I hear a loud hiss, sustained and intense. A smell comes to me, that of frying bacon and my stomach growls like a disturbed, hungry dog. Crowley has denied me breakfast in his haste to get me out here to deal with the problem, and my innards are not happy about it at all.

My target is fifteen feet away, and I slow up, my back stooping, my stance now adopting that of a stalking, half-assed warrior. I raise the baton as usual anxiety makes it weigh more than it should. I prepare to bring it down as I close the distance to ten feet.

In the time it takes for me to finish a few more paces, the man has grabbed his rifle and is on one knee, the muzzle aimed at my head.

CHAPTER FIVE

"You make more noise than a pair of mating foxes," he says from behind his beard. As well as his rifle he has both eyes on me, I suspect that at this range he could have shut them and still send my brains into the trees.

Yet this is not what has me gasping in shock. "You *heard* me?"

The man grunts. "Yeah. I heard you."

He climbs to his feet, the rifle remaining butted into his shoulder. He is tall, well over six feet. "Where's your handler?"

I shook my head. "I don't know what—"

The gun roars and the screech of protesting birds as they lift skywards is deafening. In amongst the chaos I hear a short sharp cry, recognising it as Crowley.

I hear the shuffling sounds of someone staggering through the underbrush and turn to see my captor stumble from behind some bushes. His hands clutch his stomach, where a splash of deep crimson blossoms. Rivulets run across his fingers and I think of Poppy eating ice cream in the park as raspberry juice smatters a new party dress.

Crowley's eyes are wide, but they appear to see nothing, they have a glaze to them, and his mouth hangs slack. He collapses and lies still, and I slowly turn back toward the man who has killed him, expecting the gunshot to come before I complete the cycle.

"Guess I have to think about what I'm going to do with you," the man says. "Seems a shame to waste a bullet. Maybe I can take that baton you got there and beat you to death? That was your intention, right?"

I look down at the baton, aghast that I'm still holding on to it like it has any further part to play in this façade. I drop it on the floor as if it has suddenly morphed into a live snake.

"No. It wasn't me; you understand?" I jerk my head towards the body across the clearing. "Crowley made me do things for him." I sound pathetic.

The man nods at my leg. "He do that?"

"Yeah. To make sure I couldn't stray too far."

The man sighs. "They're pretty desperate, I guess. Doesn't mean it's right. But I get it."

The words came out of me before I can process their risk. "You going to kill me?"

"I should," he says but there is no faith to his words. "Or at least beat your ass senseless with that stick of yours. But I got bacon to eat, and neither you nor your handler is going to interrupt that, get me?"

I use silence to demonstrate acquiescence.

He drops the rifle to his hip; the muzzle still follows my lead. "Go and sit opposite me. You can either have a bellyful of bacon or bullets, your choice."

I sit down, the movement clumsy, and I wince as I stretch out my leg.

The man waits until I'm seated before he, too, sits. He rests the rifle in his lap. The bacon cooks in a flat pan of grease as he takes a small spoon and flips the rashers over.

"At least this interruption hasn't burned my breakfast," he mutters. "That's very good news for you, my friend. You got a name?"

"Chris. You?"

He pauses and looks at me with eyes of deep brown. Moving his heavy fringe off his weathered face, I note that the crease lines under his lids and carved into his cheeks are deep. "You can call me Paul," he says with a grin.

One of his canines is missing.

I nod, uncomfortable in the silence that follows. "So, do we shake hands, or what?"

"No. You just stay right there. Then I won't have to shoot you before breakfast."

I stay put. Even new habits die hard, I now realise.

***

Paul burps and wipes grease from his lips. "Shit, that was good. Can't beat a bit of cured pig, right?"

I can't disagree. And not just because of the gun. We've had six rashers each and used stale bread, softened by the grease to bulk out the meal. Paul is relaxed. It makes me nervous that he can kick back when only half an hour ago he'd killed a man. I guess that is what it is like out in the world now: shoot first, live later.

I watch him pull a Zippo and a carton of cigarettes from one of the many pockets of his rucksack. He pops one of his fags into the corner of his mouth and sparks up. He makes no attempt to offer me one. Doled bacon and sparing bullets aside, there seems to be some limit to his generosity after all.

I wait as he draws on his cigarette. "So, are you from around here?"

He blows out smoke, slowly—deliberately—as though savouring each second. "Shit no," he says eventually. "This is the countryside. Give me brick walls and concrete any day."

"So how come you're in the middle of a wood?"

He clucks his tongue and smiles. "It's a fair point you're making. But the city life isn't what it used to be, right? Not for the likes of us hearing folk. Staying is a good way to get tasered and leashed. Poor bastards have lost their way and are desperate to find it again."

I look down at my leg. "Yeah. At what cost?" I make no attempt to hide my bitterness.

"You think you're the only one who lost something? Aren't you the martyr?" He chuckles.

A quiet anger joins the bacon and bread in my gut. "Sounds like you got a lot of sympathy yet you're quick enough to shoot a man."

"Didn't shoot *you*, did I?" Paul winks. "I got sympathy for them. But I care more about me. And mine."

I know what he implies. The world had become less about cohesion and inclusion and more the hearing and the deaf. 'Us and Them' made so real a man could be shot for it.

"Seems irrational, doesn't it?" Paul says as he peers into flame dancing over kindling. "But things are black and white these days. A deaf handler wants to hedge their bets out in the world. And to do that they need people like us. Hearing or not, I intend to stay a free man. Which means, living in shitholes like this."

"Doesn't have to be that way, now." I am cautious how I broach this issue. He still has the gun and I'm still not clear if he intends to put me in the ground alongside Crowley. "We have the farm."

Paul laughs. "We going to play happy family, you and me?" To my surprise he shakes his head. "I've already got a place to go."

These words put a flutter of panic in my chest. It's an age since I have been in the company of someone who is like me. Despite killing Crowley and how short a time he has been in my life, I see Paul as kindred. His actions have changed everything, my gaoler is gone and so is my prison. I can choose to stay here where everything is safe and familiar, recycle the security protocols taught to me by Crowley and live here for as long as I can.

I try to articulate this prospect while Paul stubs his cigarette out on the damp undergrowth. "Why would you want to continue living out in the wilds when there's a perfectly good place here?"

"Were you in real estate before the world turned bad?"

"What I'm saying is it makes no sense to put yourself at more of a risk than you already are. Is it because you don't trust me? I get that, but—"

As Paul adjusts his position and holds up a hand to stop me. The rifle dips to the floor. I wonder if it is a conscious act, one of acceptance that I really wasn't much of a threat after all. His eyes fall upon mine, and in those dark spots, I see only sadness.

"I appreciate your offer, really I do," he says. "Even if only forty minutes ago you tried to put a baton across my head! I think that you're trustworthy. I can see that in folk, it's a gift I've had long before all of this shit."

"Then why?"

"I'm following something," Paul says and for the first time he pulls his voice to a whisper.

If there is any doubt left in him about my intention to do him no harm, then it becomes manifest seconds later when he lays the rifle on the ground. He reaches into his pack and when he brings out the object from the canvas's folds, I gasp as though he has produced Aladdin's Lamp.

In his hands, Paul holds a radio.

My voice wavers in awe. "You're looking for The Refuge?"

He raises his eyebrows in surprise and leans forward, eyes expectant.

"You know where it is?"

I shake my head.

He deflates a little. "Well, I guess that would've been a little too easy."

"I have the co-ordinates."

"Likewise, Chris. I'm getting lazy in my old age. Maybe because I'm sick of everything being a chore. So, yes, the thought of staying here is a temptation, there's no denying it. But as much as I'd like to stay and get to know you without the baton, I want to be around people, lots of people. And, yes, it's going to be heavy going to find The Refuge. But this," he tapped the radio, "this makes the steps a little bit lighter, right?"

I didn't want to use the 'H' word, but he is right. The voice in the radio did indeed give some light in these dark days.

"Can I come with you?"

He casts his eyes over Crowley's Gift. "Don't know. I need to move fast when the occasion calls. You might slow me down."

I feel his reticence before the words come to me. I press on. "I'll do a deal. If I slow you down, then you just go. I'll catch up. We're going to the same place. You'll just get there before me."

"I have no idea if I'm going to even make it. And that's with two good legs and a rifle."

I try to diffuse the pleading tone in my response. It's tough going. "At least let me *try*?"

Paul looks at me. The seconds roll out, their passing punctuated by the cracking campfire.

"Okay," he finally says. "But first I got a question."

"Okay."

"Got any booze?"

I think about Crowley's hooch before I reply. "No."

***

I bury Crowley next to his wife, much to Paul's bemusement. He leans with his shoulder against the trunk of a tree, those dark eyes watching as I first drag my captor's corpse out of the woods, a ruddy smear on the lichen and moss marking our passage, and then again as I place

Crowley's arms across his chest, the early onset of rigor mortis making the joints creak and pop as I manoeuvre the limbs into place.

"That piece of shit would be put to better use feeding crows," Paul laughs.

"This is for *me*, not him." I begin to search for rocks to build the cairn. "Enough of what I was has gone."

Paul reacts by falling silent, leaving the birds and breeze the space to do their thing. I understand his reticence, but I mean what I say, the past few years have been acid, stripping away the man I was, the values defining my identity. To some extent I am accepting of this but the intrinsic of *being* is something I cling to like the guilt of a disaster survivor. Integrity, and humanity, are all I have left, and I intend to exercise them where and when I can.

Paul's actions—the wry smile and nonchalant demeanour—are hallmarks of just how fruitless he considers such deeds. His weathered clothes and skin are his statement to the world and its horrors.

It dawns on me, as I pile rocks on Crowley's corpse, that I will soon know the same world from which I have been cocooned for so long. I saw it many seasons ago when I made my way from my village to watch Rose get hauled away to Cathedral.

Christ knows how bad it is now.

For a moment, a quiet fear quivers in my chest, and it crosses my mind that the farmhouse may not have been a prison at all, but a fortress from the hostile lands upon which I will soon walk.

CHAPTER SIX

I test the weight of the backpack and an involuntary groan fills the farm kitchen. As this is all new to me, I have packed for most eventualities, but the most important thing—my figure of eight radio—is in a side pocket, kept near like a precious keepsake.

"You sure you got enough stuff, chief?" Paul muses. "You're going have to hump that pack for God-knows how many miles."

"I'll manage," I say as I put the pack down on the floor.

"You're going to have to, lad. I'm getting too old for piggybacks."

The pause is brief before the room fills with our laughter. The joke is poor by anyone's standard but we double over regardless to its merit, the tears in my eyes are, for once in a long, long time, the product of joy, and I go with it, welcoming it, bathing in all its inane, rib-aching glory.

The guffaws fade and we are both left panting like a weekend jogger. The adrenaline leaves my hands trembling and my head light. But the feeling is good, and I go with it.

Paul breaks rank and ends the ambience. "We'll wait until night; the dark is our best friend on this trip."

I go to the woodstove, where the heat is manifest in the deep red embers beyond the glass plate. I pull a pan from the racks overhead and place it on the hob.

"Then I guess we've got time to eat."

The smile comes back to my saviour's face. "Always."

***

"Son of a bitch."

Paul is checking over Crowley's rifle which he's retrieved from the woods. The black surface is slick like wet Tarmac and Paul has it laid out on his lap as he sits at the table.

"What is it?"

"Firing pin is gone."

"That mean it's broken?"

"Means it's *deactivated*," Paul says with a smile. "But yes, your handler was hoping the day would never come when he'd have to use this beauty. It's fucking useless."

"Bastard." It is muttered and pretty much sums up my life here at the farm. A charade from start to finish.

However, the bitterness does not linger, and this takes me by surprise. Contentment settles over me with such ease, I am at first unsure of its motives. It has been some time since I have had this warm feeling draping over me like a comfort blanket. Although I am not accustomed to it, I know why it has paid me a visit.

There is the radio and there is Paul. There is the promise of a life beyond the walls of Crowley's fake world, the road trip of salvation. Compared to what has been lost, these elements are, on the surface, token but they are all I have left. These days, anything that gives semblance of a sense of purpose is as much a valued service as being able to hear.

"Seems we have a day to kill," Paul says. "Don't know about you, Chris, but I could sleep for England."

"Feel free to use any of the beds upstairs."

"What about you?"

"Think I'll use the sofa."

"If you insist."

Paul heads off up the stairs and I remain seated at the table, my smile only slipping to accommodate a sip of tea.

***

Paul gets up as dusk begins to make its case on the landscape. I have dozed for most of the afternoon, but overall, I have basked in my newfound freedom. The farmhouse is different without Crowley, my life is different. The atmosphere has lost its oppressive, sombre air, like the cool breeze after the thunderstorm.

Dinner is a meal of tinned steak and kidney pie and dehydrated mashed potatoes, and canned peas. I wash this down with tea (though Paul has coffee) and powdered milk.

There's so much I want to ask but our discussion through dinner is that of strangers chatting at a bus stop, cordial and non-intrusive.

We finish our meal and gather our kit, stowing it in the hall as we have one final check that we have what we need.

I go to the water purifier and pour us a cup of water each, handing one to Paul.

"A toast," I say. "To roads not travelled."

"Amen."

Paul empties his cup and places it in the drainer. "So, are we getting out of here today, or what?"

"Damn right."

But he's already pulling on his pack, fedora in place and heading for the front door.

He doesn't look back.

***

We walk steadily, yet with caution, through the woods, our torches turning branches and bracken to stark, skeletal streaks. In places, the boughs entwine giving the impression of a vast web of some great arachnid waiting to drop from the sky and, after pumping venom into our soft bodies with rigid fangs, snatch us away.

The landscape ahead changes, the oaks thin out, thousands of stars bristle against the inky backdrop, bleeding through the space between rows of trunks. We move, the ground beneath our feet rising into a slight incline. Making our way forwards, the tree line becomes more defined.

Crowley's Gift click-clacks, setting the pace like a half-arsed metronome. We are only a mile from the farmhouse and my knee is griping. I have no intention of letting on, Paul has made clear there's no allowance once committed to the task. The choice I have made begins and ends at Paul's campfire. If there's any going back, then I'm well and truly on my own.

So, I press on, as shackled to vestiges of hope as I am to the cruel device strapped to my leg and keeping me stable.

At this second, climbing over the stile that marks the exit from Crowley's land, I'll take stability (mental and physical) anywhere I can find it.

I place both feet on the ground, my back leaning against the stile, my eyes behind closed lids as I take in great snorts of air. Paul's voice is suddenly in my ear.

"You enjoying that?"

I open my eyes; my companion's face is leering into view like a campfire storyteller in the torchlight.

"Yeah, I am."

"So you should," he says with sudden seriousness in his voice. "I find the air always smells sweeter as a free man."

***

The unkempt landscape beyond the boundary line is at odds with carefully tended allotments I'm used to since life with Crowley. In many ways it helps me to instantly take stock of my current place in the world, a cosseted captive, earning ignorance as much as protection from the changes beyond our borders.

And it is not just the landscape where change is tangible. We pass several vehicles as we walk. They are parked neatly at the side of the road, as though owners had alighted for a picnic in the surrounding countryside, but never made it back. Over time, the land has staked its claim upon them, weeds climbing up the tyres before crawling across the body work, machines cocooned inside twisting green strands, showered with flowers turned yellow by our torch beams.

I pause beside a grey hatchback. "Perhaps we could make things easier and see if one of these cars still works?"

"Also makes it easier for people to spot us. Cars need roads, Samaritans *use* roads. Those folks are deaf not stupid. Let's avoid anything that has us bumping into any of them. Agreed?"

"Agreed."

I concede to logic but inside I remain anxious. The openness of our surroundings makes me feel exposed, vulnerable. I recall Crowley sitting in the rain, looking out for cars on the roads, and Paul's words gain power. So, despite my reservations I follow Paul as he continues ahead.

Without a vehicle, our progress is slow going on account of Crowley's Gift. Throughout it all, Paul is brooding yet patient, and occasionally we break into conversation, about lives before the infection, moments of light in the omnipotent darkness, that eventually seemed to serve no other purpose but to remind us of what we've lost.

For long periods of time we say nothing, our passage through the dark, silent world marked only by the squeaks and clunks of Crowley's Gift, and the night calls of unseen animals.

Periodically we stop for a break, always some distance away from the road, using tall, unruly grass or dense woodland for cover. During these times we use Paul's radio, and listen to the mesmerising voice of our incorporeal belle, using it as inspiration for our journey.

CHAPTER SEVEN

We're ten miles out when we come across the body. Until this point my first hours of freedom have been uneventful. The road we walk upon is the A38, the main tributary to Birmingham, which is currently twelve miles behind us, and now known as Cathedral.

The re-christening of Birmingham is based on the nature of its rebirth, though it has about as much to do with righteousness as Margaret Atwood's *Gilead*. In the city's cathedral, the last survivors of MNG-U took consensus and decided to overwhelm the few hearing people amongst their number and place them under the yoke. Thus, the emasculation of the hearing began, but it also gave rise to something equality as sinister.

Social order at a price.

The body hanging from a nearby lamppost has been there some time. It bears the usual vestiges of retribution, hands tied together above a head covered by a hood of sackcloth, the legs and torso cocooned in swathes of fabric, bound together with electrical tape. The material is gouged in places where the crows have become too impatient to wait for the wrists to flay under the weight and allow gravity to do the rest.

There is a wooden plaque about the effigy's neck. The single word scrawled across it is both statement and crime, the misspelling an indicator of the ignorance behind it.

HARBRINGER!

I wink out and there is no longer a streetlight with a body hanging from it. Instead, I am back in my classroom and standing by the media wall watching as a small boy sits at a desk as he robustly colours a circle with a bright, orange crayon on stark white card. Concentration has turned his face to stone, his mouth is an inclined hyphen, but the tip of his tongue emerges from the corner of his lips, a red strawberry that almost matches the colour of his hair.

Tim Muller has been in my class for over nine months and it is during this time that I have learned the intricacies of British Sign Language, or BSL to use the vernacular. I have managed Stage 2 and can pretty much communicate enough with the boy to be able to understand him without an interpreter, although there is always one present to make sure he is not disadvantaged in his learning. I'm destined to be his form tutor for another three years before he moves on, and during that time I will become fluent, with frequent visits to Deaf Club where I enjoy a pint and sign away the evenings as I become infused with Deaf Culture.

I wonder where Tim is now, and my heart feels heavy as I think of the effigies hanging from their lampposts, and those in trees leading up to Cathedral. Harbingers come in all shapes and sizes, all ages, but the mode of disposal is always the same. Retribution is as indiscriminate as the disease that turned mankind into monsters, poisoned by hate.

Paul's voice intrudes into the memory. "Hey, Chris, time to return to Earth."

I'm back in the street, looking up at a testament to brutality and intolerance. I shake my head but feel the need to articulate my disbelief of long standing.

"Why do they blame them?"

Paul is silent for a few seconds. I figure, like me, he's trying to make sense out of it all.

"When a situation gets as fucked up as this, I guess the world needs scapegoats."

"There's no proof that Deaf people carried MNG-U."

Paul shrugs and I get the message before he says it. "Since when did facts mean anything?"

"Truth was dying before MNG-U."

His turn to nod, now. "Fake news and anti-vaccination lobby fucked plenty up, right? Hell, they walked hand in hand like unlikely lovers."

"Well, truth is a lot simpler these days," I say. "The ones the Samaritans find who can hear get the flatbed. The ones who are Deaf get the rope."

Paul sends the beam of his torch down the street, exposing brickwork and overgrown lawns.

"No disputing that. Let's get a few more miles on the clock before dawn."

As is fast becoming his MO, he walks off without waiting to see if I plan to follow.

***

Our route takes us east for a few miles before veering south. At a point in the journey my torch sputters and I must stall to change the batteries. Paul pauses ahead and scans the night, but I see nothing more than stars and deep shadow.

We turn out the junction and see a charred rectangle ahead, the light from our torches putting bright slashes onto the object. We move closer and note that our beams are picking up the edges of cracked and peeled paint. At first my eyes cannot decipher what they see and we close in as I make out the warped keys of a piano, each one so badly burned there is no defining the ebony and ivory, just the ugly, undulating scars of fire. The sight is incongruent to the setting, like Neil Armstrong making his giant leap for mankind on the lunar surface only to be confronted by a country cottage.

I use the torch to sweep the area. Nearby, there are smashed speakers, the woofers pummelled and useless. With them is a guitar turned to ragged oblivion, the wood now in splintered, skeletal pieces, demolished save for the fretboard joined to the bridge by twisted strings.

"I guess they didn't like the band." Paul sniffs the air. "This is old stuff. Nothing to worry about."

We walk on.

***

Dawn is putting a grey line on the horizon as we peel off-road and into the hedgerow on our right. The field on the other side is a tangled forest of corn stalks, through which we force our way until we are deep within its borders.

Paul stops and the rustling sounds of our excursion are replaced by ragged panting as we catch our breath.

I dig into my coat pocket and pull free a pack of ibuprofen, palming two and swallowing them dry. My knee is a dull throb—the pills, pre-emptive, the means to ensure I can still walk tomorrow.

Paul is by my side. "How goes it?"

"I'll survive."

"That's the spirit. We need to bed down here for the day."

I nod and look about us. The corn stalks create fibrous walls and I have the abrupt feeling that we are being digested in the belly of a great beast.

Paul surveys our hideout. "Best clear some space."

We move with urgency, using shoulders to collapse the undergrowth, our feet crushing flat a haphazard square that barely accommodates us and our gear. But it is enough, and we both slump to the ground, the spongy floor odd, yet comforting.

Paul opens his bag and uses his torch to see inside. Reaching in, he rummages around until he pulls free a can of tomato soup. He pops the lid and takes three glugs, his Adams's Apple pumping like a piston.

His gratuitous feeding habits make me smile. He mirrors my grin after he paws soup from his beard with a rag that may have started out as a handkerchief.

"What? It's not like we're dining at The Ritz is it?"

I delve into my own pack and retrieve a can of beans. "Yeah, I guess fine dining's a thing of the past."

"Your past, maybe. I never had any stay at a fancy hotel and three-figure bills to pay."

I pause. Despite being tired, I'm suddenly intrigued to know more about Paul in the world that was. "So, what *did* you have?"

"You mean what did I *lose*."

I shuffle in my makeshift seat, my embarrassment given form. Paul comes to my rescue as he continues to speak, his tone flat and without vigour.

"You going to ask, or what?"

Paul's eyes sparkle in the torchlight.

"Huh?"

"Ask about me," he explains. "I've seen the look in your eyes and your mouth flapping like a stickleback in a kid's fishing net."

Paul is a mind reader.

"Okay, you got me." I smile as I admit the obvious. "Want to tell me a bit about yourself?"

"Feels like the start of an interview but yeah, I'll spill seeing as we're walking the same road."

He retrieves the canteen strapped to his pack and takes a few glugs. Then he rests his back against the corn-stalk partition.

"You want to do twenty questions, or do you want *Once Upon a Time*?"

"We've plenty of time," I offer. "But as it's about you, I guess it's up to you how you tell it."

He mulls this over and finally nods. "Okay. Let's get into it. We could be dead tomorrow."

I wish I could challenge his assessment but that would be as foolhardy as denying there's a fire when you can already see the flames eating your boots.

"Where you from?"

"Blackwell, Worcestershire."

"Town?"

"Village. A social club and church. I spent more time in one than the other."

"Which one?"

Paul laughs. "That's a trick question, right?"

I chuckle, relishing the sound of our mirth. "How long you been on the road?"

My question douses our merriment.

"Four months, maybe more."

"You set out alone?"

"Yeah. There was nothing to stay for in the end."

"Sorry."

"Like I've already said, no one's got a monopoly on loss, Chris."

The silence rolls out and I draw it to a close with another question.

"What did you do, before all of this shit?"

"Electrician. Own business. Mostly contracted work, construction companies. Brought in good money but not the sort that put me up in nice hotels." He winks, a peace offering before he continues. "You know, there's nothing as eternal as electricity. Nature will be making it long after we're gone. You just look up at the heavens in a lightning storm and everything we ever made seems so damn pointless."

"Except family," I say.

"Yeah, family is the thing we do best. But we're also good at fucking that up if we lose what's important."

"And what's that?"

"The capacity for loyalty."

"I'll drink to that."

We toast the edict with metallic tasting water from our respective canteens.

"Shall we see if Radio Refuge is transmitting?" Paul now has the radio in his hand and cranks up the battery.

He settles back, using the rucksack as a pillow. I follow suit as we both listen to the static hiss from the plastic grille.

It is the sound that will follow me into my dreams.

CHAPTER EIGHT

The hiss from the frying pan fills the kitchen. I watch as Evie prods eggs with a spatula and the air is heavy with the smell of olive oil. As she watches the pan, she talks, and her voice is like silk against the harshness from the sizzling oil.

"Do you *have* to work today? What's the point of being your own boss if you can't give yourself a day off?"

The iMac under my fingers becomes intrusive and I look up to see Evie scoop the eggs from pan, holding them for a few seconds to drain, then place them on the plates beside the hob. I become aware her deep blue eyes are regarding me with interest. There is expectation there, too. Like the grease from the eggs, it oozes from her, the need for contrition; the need for her to be put first, just this once.

I concede by pushing the iMac away from me. In the pause, a bundle of high energy enters the kitchen in the form of Poppy. She is a vision of blonde curls and blue eyes and wears her favourite *Wonder Woman* t-shirt, as well as a huge, beaming smile.

"Daddy! Are you going to play with us today?"

Poppy leaps up onto my lap and her bony knees prod my thighs making me laugh and wince at the same time.

"Not if you cripple your dad before we start," I say and the comment makes Evie's shoulders relax as she turns with the breakfast plates in both hands. The smile on her face tells me I have made the right choice, whereas her eyes make plain I didn't really have any in the first place.

As Evie places the breakfast plates on the table, I hug Poppy to me. She smells of *Zoella Soak Opera* bubble bath.

"So where shall we go today?" I say into her hair.

"The park!"

"Okay, Princess, the park it is."

Poppy looks up at me, her face scrunched. She pats the image of Wonder Woman on her chest. "I'm not a *princess*, I'm a warrior!"

"Damn right you are, gorgeous. Just like Mummy."

I give Evie a conciliatory wink and Poppy giggles as she slides off my lap.

My wife raises her eyebrows, the movement subtle, hardly perceptible. It means *'You did good, Christopher Beresford. You did really good.'*

"I'm going to get my *Vans* and jacket!" Poppy yells as she scampers out of the room. I watch her go, smile so wide it makes my cheeks ache, and a heart so full of love it is a physical heat in my chest. I have never experienced such an overwhelming surge of emotion and at that moment think I never shall again.

But my conclusions are premature; I will be consumed by emotion three weeks later when my beautiful wife and sweet, innocent daughter die, bleeding in my arms.

***

Hands are grasping my clothing, shaking away the dream (memory). I open my eyes and Paul looms over me, concern putting deep rumples into his gnarled brow.

"What is it?" I sit up and Paul's hand is still limp on my shoulder.

"You were crying in your sleep, Chris. Bad dreams?"

I touch my cheeks and my fingers come away wet. "I wish they *were* just dreams."

Tears are falling now; I make no attempt to stem their flow. Paul sits beside me and his arm is about my shoulder, his voice sombre.

"Don't we all, friend. Don't we all."

***

The day passes without much ado. A few times we hear the distant rumble of engines from the east, where the remnants of Cathedral and its maleficent guardians dwell. But there is nothing but the sounds of the countryside keeping our company until nightfall and we feel confident enough to move on.

We plan to continue south. Paul has cranked up the radio and the voice of our guide crackles in the air, encouraging us to leave our haven in the cornfield. Even though we have been in the field for a mere twelve hours, the unyielding tarmac beneath our feet seems strange.

As we did the previous night, we follow the road as it snakes off ahead. The darkness is facilitated by heavy clouds that mask the three-quarter moon I know is overhead. There is freshness to the air, and I know it will rain even before the first spots hit my coat, giving off tiny clicks. I pull up the hood of my cagoule as the fat drops plop onto my head, soaking my hair in mere moments.

The formulaic structures of a row of houses lie ahead, and I point to them as the rainstorm puts streaks in our torch beams.

"Let's take shelter," I call but Paul shakes his head, a veil of water streaming from the brim of his fedora.

"We go further up the road," he says. "These houses are too exposed to anyone in the street."

I don't argue because what he says makes sense. The Samaritans are night-shy but there's no point in tempting fate. The raindrops are now a barrage of moist ordnance which explode all over the pavements. The undergrowth that has pushed though the paving slabs shivers and glistens before us.

We pass the row of houses, their windows black, dead eyes; brick and mortar corpses of a world no longer relevant. Their gardens are small jungles, the trees rising from within the tangled mane of grass are tall, shaggy sentinels standing guard over these suburban mausoleums.

Hurrying through the downpour we see the terrace ends in a road. Another row of houses continues ahead but there is a left-hand turn leading to more dwellings. We take the corner and soon find ourselves in an estate of detached and semi-detached houses, their unkempt appearance no different from those we have already seen. Paul continues deeper into the estate, his torch sweeping the urban landscape.

We hear the growling seconds before my torch beam reflects the twin orbs of something low on the ground, a hundred yards away.

The thing scuttles forward, and my heart feels as though a cold hand has reached out and grabbed it.

CHAPTER NINE

Our torches pick out the crawling shape that edges closer, a thing of slick, wet fur and bared teeth, that collaborates with the shadows.

"What the fuck is it?" My voice is terse and shrill.

"Dog. Doberman, maybe."

"It's stalking us."

"We've all got to eat."

As practical as this observation is, it's not helping.

I start to back up, the rain and the open road suddenly have great appeal. My retreat is impeded by the patter of multiple paws behind me.

"Shit, shit, shit."

I turn to look upon what I already know to be there: a mangy, snarling mass, multiple eyes made white by my trembling torch.

There is a gunshot, it sounds like a bomb going off, and the flicker-flash of light from over my shoulder, coupled with the pitiful yelp, informs me that Paul is taking no chances.

Just as I am hoping that the rifle blast is going to have the same effect on the dog-pack as a starting pistol on a field of marathon runners, the creatures ahead hold fast, not even flinching at the sound.

Instead they crawl forward, their bellies low to the ground, dogs of all kinds, I count at least ten, but their growls come as one reverberating gurgle, a monotone menace biding its time.

"They're not scared of us."

"Time to get off the street."

"I can't run." The panic in my voice puts emphasis to the most obvious of facts.

"If you don't want to end up a dog's dinner, you'd better try."

Helplessness surges through me as the realisation that I'm still in the grasp of Crowley's cruel legacy hits home. Part of me wishes that I had heeded Paul's advice and left Crowley for the crows.

Here comes the rage, of what he did to me, the emotional abuse that has changed the way I think about the world as well as the visceral impact of his hammer. With this burning anger comes the spinning realisation that now I am free of my tormentor, I want to live; I want to return to the person that can love and be loved.

Paul's tight voice hisses in my ear. "I'll buy us some time." He raises the rifle and takes aim. "Go on the gunshot."

Now Paul is beside me, the barrel of the rifle a vision of black metal and rivulets of rainwater. I begin backing away as his shoulder leans into the stock, managing to take several steps before Paul discharges the weapon.

"Now move!" he calls.

It is true I cannot run, but I make a great attempt at lolloping at speed. In my mind, three images flit like pages of a book caught in the wind. The first is the lead dog—a bedraggled Alsatian, I think—slumping to the floor as Paul's rifle puts it down. The second is the sight of some of the pack launching themselves at their fallen comrade, frenzied teeth ripping into fur and flesh.

The third image is not of this time, it is 1994, the year Nelson Mandela is elected president of South Africa and the Channel Tunnel is officially opened by Queen Elizabeth II, becoming the umbilical between the UK and Europe. It's the school summer fete and I'm 10 years old, running the three-legged race, tied to Danny Bonas, my best friend, sweat on our brows, and the rest of the field of puffing, grunting participants. I recall the stitch in my side, the dryness in my throat. But most of all I crave the exhilaration of being so young and so fucking free.

And this is how it is now, hobbling at pace, dead Danny no longer secured to my leg, just Crowley's Gift in all its clicking, clanking glory. But the exhilaration does not come from the desire to win a poxy, plastic medal, it comes from a very real need to stay alive.

Again, I am brought back to basics—despite everything I have lost, instinct to remain on this godforsaken earth is my driver.

Behind me, there are more gunshots, more canine yelps as Paul lays down the groundwork for any kind of advantage. I can hear the patter of feet on the asphalt, but they are tiny, sounding more like the click of claws than the pad of work boots.

I make out a low wall and a tangle of trees ahead of me, and the thought that I need to get off open ground becomes overwhelming. And now there is a growl behind me, a low, aircon warble heralding images of teeth and saliva.

I can't look back; I *won't* look back. I choose to plough on, throwing myself at the wall, over the wall, leaving myself to the mercy of brambles and bricks. I feel the privet yield, the tangled undergrowth on the other side receives me with an embrace that is sharp with thorns, its caress leaves my clothes and exposed flesh snagged and torn, making me cry out, my hands and cheeks now hot, branded by nature.

I'm on all fours, a ridiculous, lame parody of the beasts hunting me down. My rucksack is askew, the weight pulling me to the left and as I come up to my good knee to compensate for the harness, a large shape crashes through the hedge knocking me flat. The wind is expelled from my lungs, my torch goes spinning off into the tangled gloom where it stops, the beam exposing the true nature of the intruder, a Rottweiler clambering to its feet and shaking away the pain its dramatic entrance has inflicted upon its body.

The growl is back in its throat and the torchlight turns its teeth into jagged yellowed daggers. I scramble for the torch, hoping to turn it into a baton but I sense movement as the dog comes for me, its shadow looming over my prone body like a cloud moving across a waxen moon. Grasping the torch, I raise my arm and swing it in an arc, trying to convince myself that it's going to connect with the Rottweiler's huge head.

All I find are the teeth. They clamp down on my forearm like a mantrap. My scream is loud and prolonged, a banshee shriek I never thought possible to emit.

The pain is immense, a pulse of agony that clouds my consciousness.

Then I'm yanked forwards, the dog now on its belly, dragging me downwards like I'm its plaything. But there's no fun to be had, only burning agony in my arm and the muffled, savage growls of my four-legged assailant.

The gnawing torment blurs my vision on a scene already muted by streaking rain and the gloom. My free hand balls into a fist and strikes out, a sequence of clumsy blows that make haphazard contact with the dog's head and snout. Ultimately these pathetic attempts at self-preservation are as ineffective as they are futile. But I continue, my knuckles finding hard ridges of the beast's brow and muzzle, jarring my hand.

When I begin slapping the brute to save my aching knuckles, my palm finds the curve of an eye socket and instinct does the rest, my thumb curling into the orbital cavity, finding the soft, yielding tissue of its eyeball and I push with all my might.

The howl of agony is pitiful and exquisite, jaws parting enough for me to pull my arms free as the great head retreats. I clutch the injured arm to my chest as the Rottweiler shakes its head trying to rid itself of the terrible hurt that I have inflicted upon it.

I am on my feet now, having grabbed the torch *en route*, but my gait is unsteady. The dog senses me, anger and fury and hunger are its motivating triad for another assault. It leaps, mouth agape, saliva and ocular goo glistening in the torch beam.

Once more I am bowled over, and I go down, my head striking something hard, and my wavering vision is filled with the oscillating image of teeth and blood. Great paws land on my chest, pinning me to the ground, making me gasp as air is forced from my lungs.

I make a token attempt to fend off the jaws, my uninjured hand grabbing the thick neck, pushing upwards. Panic arrives as I feel consciousness slipping. I don't won't to die, I want to be safe and free and alive. I want to see the owner of the voice of salvation that comes through the grille of a cheap plastic radio.

Another sound interrupts my failing thoughts, a thwack and a hiss.

Something strikes the animal towering over me and it collapses, the weight of it squeezing what little air is left in my body. My brain decides to take timeout and gradually I fade, not once expecting to ever return.

CHAPTER TEN

I come to with a start, regretting it instantly as the movement sends a bolt of pain through my brain, and a wave of nausea flips my stomach. With eyes burning like brands against lids squeezed shut; my curses come as whispers over dry, cracked lips.

My cheeks and brow sting, and I have a vague memory of getting scratched by a hedge but that is as hard as my mind is prepared to work. Fog replaces any further attempts at recall.

After a few seconds masquerade as eternity, the headache eases and I risk opening my eyes. The light is subtle, making me brave enough to ease into a squint, yet is like a solar flare at the back of my eyes, only the pain of it is brighter.

Determined, I blink several times, desensitising my wits to the worldview and so it is the scene unfolds, defused by bloody-mindedness if nothing else.

I'm in a small lounge, mauve walls and dull, cream skirting-boards. There is an armchair and sofa opposite, gaudy. Pink leather things with fluffy, red scatter cushions. The armchair is vacant but on the sofa is a young woman. I figure she is in her late teens, black hair tied back from her coffee-cream face, ink-well eyes unwavering.

In her lap I see the slingshot, fashioned from metal and moulded blue plastic. In the leather pouch there is a steel sphere that has a sparkling corona. The ball bearing is pinched between her thumb and index finger, ready and waiting for me to start to get clever.

I suck in air and my brain begins to respond by helping me see straight. The girl wears a t-shirt and her bare arms are festooned with animal tattoos. On her right arm, I see a tiger crawling out from beneath the t-shirt and merge into an illustrated sleeve of big cats featuring a panther, a lion and a leopard. From the left sleeve, I see a rabbit, a gazelle, a zebra and ibex.

But despite this living tapestry, I am drawn to one image. It is displayed proudly on her left wrist and consists of a blue laurel cupping three concentric circles, the innermost with five stars—red, yellow, green, blue and black—positioned clockwise, and at the centre three interlocking circles making it look like a biohazard symbol.

I know this mark well. It belongs to the World Federation of the Deaf, established in Rome in 1951 and one of the oldest international organisations for those with disability. The WFD fought for human rights and lobbied policy-makers worldwide to remove barriers for those ostracised by ignorance.

I recall attending one of their conferences in London ten years ago; around the time I met Tim. The pride, the passion for a culture defined by what those outside would consider an infirmity. A knot sits in my stomach, these days the Deaf are considered Harbingers of the silent apocalypse, guilty without proof or trial.

The look in her eyes as she regards me from the hideous sofa tells me she thinks this whole thing sucks, too. Yet the stare says something else, it says: *"I intend to push back against persecution, I intend to survive."*

I decide to bridge the divide, make peace in the silence.

It is as I try to lift my hands into position to facilitate discourse, I realise they are bound to arms of my chair with swatches of silver duct tape. The movement sends a flare of pain through my right forearm and I grimace, air hissing through teeth clenched so tightly they begin to squeak like cornered church mice.

My right arm is a patchwork of neatly applied bandages. My wrist has a bracelet of matt-silver tape that holds me fast to the chair. I test my feet and they are as equally immobile. I imagine they, too, have duct tape manacles.

As I test my bonds, the girl across the room shuffles forwards, the sling shot now raised and primed. It is a warning, a statement that I should stop any thoughts of fucking her over. I take heed and slump into my chair; an appeasing gesture I hope she takes in good faith.

For several seconds she still holds my head in the sights of the slingshot. I imagine that ball bearing hitting my forehead at speed, putting the lights out for good as my brain leaks through my ears. I stay respectfully still but my mind is greased and gearing up, churning through the 'what-ifs and maybes' that has my infernal love of life stoking the pot.

I bend the wrist of my left hand, my index and middle finger adopting a pistol point to the ceiling and putting an imaginary tick on the air. This is followed by my index finger waving like a metronome, thumb and other digits balled into my palm.

Name what?

It is a simple sign but the reaction in the face of the girl opposite is a complex mix of surprise and suspicion. To my relief, she lowers the slingshot.

I repeat the sign, trying to avoid my frustration as it overspills into the delicate nuances of gesture and expression.

Name what?

The girl tilts her head and her hands rise to the occasion; the slingshot poised in her lap. She puts two fingers beneath her right ear, eyebrows raised in query before dropping her hand and pointing at me as she clucks a tiny response.

Deaf you?

I gently shake my head, unsurprised by her confusion. I form a platform with my fingers and jab them forward twice.

Teacher.

She nods as if this now makes sense, asking me if I can still hear and it is now my turn to nod. As I make the sign for help—a thumb up and pulled towards me as best as the tape allows, the action causes me to groan with pain.

She leans forwards, elbows resting on knees, her eyes watching every move in my face.

She finger-spells SHELLY and it is fast. But I was good at what I did, and I have Tim Muller to thank for my skill. In

2003 British Sign Language was recognised by the government as the fourth indigenous language of the UK.

Who knew it was soon to be the only language of relevance?

The irony was that for so many years the Deaf Community had been dissuaded from using the very language defining their culture, given form in the capitalised 'D' in Deaf when related to themselves. Like most minorities, the Deaf have been the victims of abuse at the hands of the ignorant. They've suffered repression and medicalisation as the hearing world felt they needed to be curtailed and cured.

During my time on Deaf Awareness courses I learned that the Deaf language was outlawed in western schools, hands caught signing were beaten with canes. The education system of the hearing was imposed on the Deaf in the 19th century and the only lesson learned was illiteracy. At one time, debates were held as to the efficacy of stopping the spread of the affliction by preventing Deaf couples from marrying and reproducing. All of it considered reasonable in the quest to prevent an epidemic.

The thought makes me ashamed, the actualities more so.

The baseline was always about deafness as disability. In truth, I know the Deaf Community does not see their deafness as nothing short of empowerment. Deafness *is* their culture, the very reason for their being.

I also know they don't want to be 'cured' by science, they want to live, to be accepted for who they are and what they can contribute. Before MNG-U, inroads were being made, schools had BSL on their curriculum, sign language interpreters were standard on TV and at major venues, and Oscar-winning movies raised awareness to the masses.

I used to think history was barbaric but, Jesus Christ, what happens to the Deaf today makes the treatments of old appear like a fucking spa day.

Then came MNG-U, and the inroads became overrun with the twisted logic of hate and fear. After the infection came the festering poison that ultimately affected any semblance of a rational mind. As Paul said, the world needs a focus of its ills, after all.

I can't say that I see this in the girl sitting opposite. Yes, she has the slingshot and yes, I'm under no doubt she could—and would—use it if she felt I was straying from the path of truth. But there is irony in the fact that we are both natural fugitives in this world of slaves and exiles. And it is this I see now, as she realises, I am a bridge that spans the divide, an ally in rebellion.

If I need confirmation of my theory, Shelly puts the slingshot to one side and stands. She reaches behind her back and draws a vicious-looking hunting knife. The blade is so wide, I can see my wavering shape in its stunning steel surface. Despite this positivity, for a moment I see the serrated edge putting a red line across my throat as my severed carotid artery pumps a cataract of warm claret into my lap.

The moment passes as she crouches and seems to merely touch the silver tape on my wrists and ankles with the knife and I am free. I use the time it takes for her to stand and walk back to her seat to cautiously massage my limbs. My forearm warns me not to be too reckless by sending dull agony through my nerve endings.

Shelly sheaths her knife and sits down, the slingshot remains beside her, but I sense it is now redundant. We serve no purpose to each other dead, nor is there any valid reason to be at odds.

We are each trapped by the failings the world has bestowed upon us.

***

I watch Shelly as she busies herself about the dining table. Time has moved on but at an indeterminable pace. All I know is that darkness still holds sway over the world, and we continue to sit in the twilight of small lamps that make the hideous design on the wallpaper cavort like the disciples of Satan dancing around a bonfire.

The blow to my head has left me groggy. I find that my mind tries to latch onto events that have recently happened, but they are illusive, mere shadows without substance. I'm aware that concussion does this kind of thing, but I still find it frustrating. Trying not to force things, I merely pass the time observing my host as she goes about her business with a quiet determination.

Shelly has laid the table for supper, there is a gold and glass cafetière and she has cooked up a tin of beans and powdered eggs, served up on matching white plates with fat, red flower motifs. I have figured out this is not where Shelly used to live even before I ask her. The layout and feel of the place seem old, the air perfumed with musk and the faint lavender scent that always seems to pervade the elderly. It reminds me of visiting my grandmother's house in Stafford.

The memory jars, too many years have passed by since it last paid my mind a visit. It is a thing of ambiguity; love and loss merge with disgust, an idiom for so many instances in the past few years. My heart stalls in my chest as the errant image of my grandmother escapes, for so many years it has been repressed, kept fettered and neutered in the shadowy world of stifled memories. Perhaps, with so little thought occupying my mind, there is opportunity for it to gatecrash. Irrespective of the reason, the memory is free to roam around my beleaguered skull causing nothing but heinous mischief.

I'm in my grandmother's lounge and she is peering up at me through half mast lids. Her eyes are deep brown, but exploded capillaries have turned the whites to pink, her mouth is agape as though in silent protest. So powerful is the memory, I can almost feel the cushion in my hands, a padded square of silk that I have used to snuff out a life I held so dear. Too dear to allow the pain and suffering of the latter stages of MNG-U to have its way.

Emotions swell, the image of my grandmother blurs as tears hamper my vision. Somehow, I break free of these recollections, but the tears follow me into the here and now. I paw at them with the back of my uninjured arm.

A double thump on the table has me turning away from my past crimes; Shelly is determined to get my attention and she now looks at me with the kind of concern that I've not seen for some time. I sit myself up in my seat like a child told off for slouching.

We engage in sign.

"Problem what?"

"Bad memories."

She nods, making it clear I'm not alone in such things.

"Want to talk about it?" I sign.

"I don't know you," she signs back.

It's my turn to nod given that she's not wrong. But these days not-knowing is standard.

I try to diffuse the tension with a smile. "Are you alone?"

"Are you?"

The question is like connection leads, jump-starting my brain. The memory-fog clears like it has been swept away by some gale force wind and I am at once aware of what has occurred. The image of Paul and his rifle emerge like a fucking nightmare. How the fuck could I forget about him? Realisation has grabbed me by the shoulders and shaken me awake.

"Shit!"

I clamber to my feet and Shelly pulls the slingshot as if from nowhere and I raise my left hand, palm open, a disarming gesture before signing that I have a companion who saved me from the dogs.

She lowers the slingshot, laying it on the table, not too far from reach.

"Thought I saved you?"

I sigh and look towards the drawn, heavy curtains. "You did, and I thank you for that, you know I mean it. But I have a companion—Paul—who risked his life so I could get over that hedge. I need to go and get him, see if he's okay."

Shelly's posture softens, indicating some resignation. But her response is direct. "He's dead—the dogs will have had him."

Deaf-speak is so to the point it borders on indifference. Communication without the frills. Sometimes it works, but at times such as these, subtlety becomes a casualty to syntax.

Still, I try to push back. "You can't know that for sure."

"I can. The dogs keep me safe, but they also keep me *here*." For emphasis, Shelly jabs an index finger at the ground.

"So how do you get supplies—provisions?"

"They hide during the day. Away from Samaritans and their guns. Night is their time. I leave them to it."

She drops her head and when she looks up again, I see the genuine remorse in her gaze. "I'm sorry. He's gone."

I think of Paul, out there in the dark, mauled and mangled, dragged across the pavement like some worthless carcass. Another life senselessly lost and meaningless. There is a pain in my injured arm, and I look down to see my hand gripping the back of the chair, knuckles white. I relax and sit back down, shoulder sagging as I try to shut my mind down for a while, and maybe give it time to process yet another loss.

Guilt sits with me; Paul was saving my life as he gave up his own. Another thought comes, though it is perhaps more delusion than a reality. Maybe Paul made it out of here, got hold of his radio and just headed off. Until I see a body, I can still hold on to that whimsy.

For now, it will do, it will help.

I place a palm to my forehead then run splayed fingers through my greasy hair. My quest is in doubt before it has even begun. Yes, I have my radio, but any impetus to chase dreams of a hearing utopia are shaken. Just like the dreams that were pinned to the concept. No, not pinned, slapped on with the cheapest tape on the market. Now all I have is—what?

You have your life, Chris. What more do you want? The voice of my long dead wife is in my ear. The soft, warm tones of memory but in truth, had she been alive and standing here in this dining room, the admonishment would've been edged with her usual disdain for pessimism.

She doesn't hear my sigh, but I send it out into the room regardless, and Shelly tentatively sits down opposite. She pushes something forward, her thick fingers and chewed nails guiding the object's passage across the tablecloth. Her fingers retreat and leave an item behind, reminding me of flotsam abandoned by the tide. My eyes trace the lines, marvelling at the delicate craftsmanship that that has given form to this intricate wonder.

I feel her eyes on me and look up into them. I pick up the totem, a small crab that fits easily in the centre of my palm. It's made of balsa and has no weight at all. The surface has been polished smooth and painstakingly painted in greens and blues; details that must have taken hours. I figure nothing leaves you with time on your hands quite like avoiding fanatics who want to hang you from a lamppost.

"Did you make this?"

"Stops me getting bored."

"It's beautiful."

My comment puts redness on her cheeks and neck. I spare her embarrassment by continuing as if I haven't noticed.

"So why a crab?"

"In China the crab means prosperity and high status."

I nod though I don't agree with it. High status like mine doesn't lead to prosperity, just a cage. Besides, these days, China is probably as dead as our own god-forsaken country.

Shelly is unaware of my doubts as she continues to sign, her small hands moving smoothly through the air, voice switched off making it easier for me to understand the gestures.

"This totem will give you armour and strength of purpose. It gives clarity to uncertain paths we walk. If you believe in this stuff."

"These days I'll take optimism wherever I can get it. Thank you."

Her face flushes again and she tries to hide it by turning away. Her actions show just how young she is, just how *lost*.

As though they are precious, I keep such thoughts to myself. "Thank you. For all of this, really."

"It's what people should do."

She is right but the comment brings back to me how much things have changed. And just how bad it has got. Moments like these are an oasis in a barren land so used to giving us a mirage, the false flag behind which humanity now rallies.

Shelly stands and heads for the door. She stops before going into the next room and jerks her head towards the doorway, indicating I need to follow her.

I heed her call as she disappears into the adjacent room. I take thoughts of Paul and the crab token with me, the contrast of the heavy thoughts of my new redeemer and inconsequent weight of the palmed crab-totem not lost on me, but shelved; ready to be referenced later when I am alone and trying to snuggle down under a blanket of self-pity.

This makes me remorseful.

As I follow Shelly, she moves with purpose, a testament to her desire to live whatever life she can. I wonder if this has always been the way for her, and I force myself to make note of this question and ask her about what stories she has from before MNG-U ravaged humanity. She has survived here alone for months and can still express sanguinity. I must admit that this fills me with a murky sense of envy. She has more to fear from the world beyond the windows and the pack of wild dogs. Where I have slavery, she has certain death.

I can see that the room next door was once a study or work-at-home-office. There are shelving units against the left wall where lever-arch folders of green and red stand to attention. The first thing that hits me is the sweet scent of wood, I use a cliché and follow my nose.

Under the bay window, at the far end of the room, is a desk. It's nothing special—just a flat-pack, home assembly gig—but lay upon it, amongst whittling knives, solder kit and swatches of sandpaper and emery cartouches, are creations of incredible beauty.

There are many effigies, wrought from different materials, but unified by a common theme: like her tattoos, they are all animals. There is a delicate silhouette of a rabbit no bigger than a house key, frozen in a leap, its eye made of a tiny red bead, the metal sparkles in places and I assume the material it is made from is stainless steel. Next to the rabbit there is a bear raised on its hind legs, it is bigger and made from dark wood that has been filed to an unblemished sheen. A small vice has been screwed to the desk and in its grasp is what I assume is Shelly's current work in progress, a metal cameo of a dog's head, jaws wide as though frozen mid-bark. Inside I shudder, this is a little too soon. As though in sympathy my bitten forearm throbs.

Shelly stands beside the table, shoulders pulled back in pride. The action instantly reminds me of when Poppy had shown me a haphazard picture of three descending stick figures, two with triangle-torsos and straggly, long hair, the last figure with a mid-sized moustache that seemed to want to escape its face. The memory puts a smile on my lips, but a tear traverses my right cheek. I let it fall, unimpeded, my vista spangles for a short moment and then I wipe my eyes on my sleeve as I move towards the items on the desk.

"How did this all start?"

Shelly dips her finger into the neckline of her blouse and pulls free a shoelace with a small dolphin pendant attached. She drapes it over one finger and raises it slightly, and the pendant dances on air.

"My mother. She was a sculptor."
"Did she make that for you?"
"Yes. For my tenth birthday."

I see the corners of her mouth do a jig as she fights to compose herself.

Everybody hurts, Michael Stipe once said.

Ain't that the fucking truth?

CHAPTER ELEVEN

It's later and we are sitting in the lounge, me on the heavy armchair, Shelly is back on the sofa, both of us nursing hot cups of black coffee. I take a sip; two sugars have made it bittersweet.

"What happened to your folks?" I sign.

"Same as yours, I'll bet."

Don't go there, Shelly. For God's sake, don't go there. I concede with another sip of coffee.

"Why do they hate us?" Shelly signs.

"Who?"

"The people who hang us. Why do they hate us?"

I respond quickly. "They're afraid. And angry. It makes them see things, *differently*."

Defending the Samaritans' barbaric practices makes me feel complicit. Guilt and anger bubble away inside me. Shelly becomes a distraction from a colossal sense of betrayal.

"They hurt us. We could help them. You know, help them cope."

I think this over before responding. "They don't want to accept what they've become. It's turned them sour."

"I had no choice. I had to get on with it. It's not right to blame others for what's gone wrong in your life."

I realise that these are the words of parents long since gone. I wonder what Shelly's kin looked like and how they brought up a Deaf girl in a prominently hearing world. Again, I see her vulnerability, fleeting but so absolutely there it is like a shadow upon her spirit.

"Come with me?" I say.

"Where?"

"A place in the southeast. They call it The Refuge. It has people there who want to start over. No Samaritans, no killing. No more death." Even as I say the words, I'm not sure I believe the reality of what such a place offers.

"*Hearing* people?"

"Yes."

I watch her face sag with disappointment. "There's no place for me there."

"They say it is a place for everyone. I bet they mean Deaf people, too."

"But you can't be sure. Hearing people hate Deaf people just like those in Cathedral."

I stand and take a few steps before I go down on my good knee, looking up at her like she's a deity. "No, that's not true at all. This world is just fucked up. I've a chance to get to somewhere that's as normal as its going to get."

"Then you go," she signs, the movements exaggerated as her emotions get the better of her.

To placate, I turn my palm downwards and bounce my hand on the air. "You can't stay here alone. It's only a matter of time before the Samaritans find you. Or maybe those dogs."

All through my spiel Shelly shakes her head, discordant and frenzied. She ends any chance of discourse by shutting her eyes.

I reach for her, my hand gently touching her forearm, just to get her to re-engage but her response comes so quickly I am taken by surprise.

"No!" The sound that comes from her mouth is thick but clear.

Shelly jumps up, knocking me off-balance. Instinct has my injured limb stretching out to support me and I immediately regret it as pain flares up my forearm and I cry out.

The riled youth stomps from the lounge and I hear the heavy thumps as she goes upstairs. The withdrawal ends with the slam of a bedroom door.

Cradling my arm, I return to the armchair and take solace in the coffee and the silence.

***

I wake abruptly, though there is no apparent reason for such a violent wrench from sleep. The house is quiet enough to hear each tiny creak and click as though each joist, each wall, is stretching off its slumber.

Sitting up in the chair, I'm reminded that it's been a few too many hours since I've had any painkillers. My arm smarts where teeth pinched my skin and my knee aches as though it's been exposed to the frigid elements.

Dipping my hands into the pockets of my cargo pants, I grab a blister strip of ibuprofen and pop three pills into my palm. I wash them down with the dregs of cold coffee left in the cup from the night before, grimacing in disgust.

For the next twenty minutes, as I wait for the pills to kick in, I ponder on the disagreement I've had with Shelly. I soon realise that this was always going to be a difficult sell to someone who has spent a life feeling disconnected from the majority. Even with supportive parents, society still has a propensity to snub what it does not understand. Why should today be any different?

I test out my knee. Although it is stiff, the pain is at least bearable and gingerly I stand and shamble to the kitchen, needing to rid my throat of the bitter taste of stale coffee.

It is as I grab the water jug, I see the note on the counter. The biro is laid across it like a stop sign. Heart quickening, I go over and read the neat script without picking up the paper.

It is not safe for me. You must leave. I am hiding until you go. I have put stuff in your bag to last two days. Hope you find what you're looking for.

Shelly.

Moving to the kitchen window, I see the dawn light as grey steel in the sky, too light for the dogs, too dark for the Samaritans. I figure Shelly was planning on holding out in some other building until I take my leave. The first vestiges of anger and fear come to me. I've driven her away with my overbearing desire to keep her safe. The right was not mine; I see that now. And, as always, the lesson has been learned far too late.

The silence in the kitchen reflects my growing sense of isolation. A decision is fogged by competing ideas on a way forward. Do I dig in and stay regardless of Shelly's plea? Do I go on alone and hope that I get lucky enough to evade dangers, known and unknown, and be rewarded safe harbour in the new lands of The Refuge. Or do I just turn tail and go back to Crowley's farm to live out the rest of this damned life praying the scent traps forever keep the Samaritans at bay?

My head spins, my stomach lurches. I realise anxiety is pumping my lungs and I'm hyperventilating. Sucking in air, I hold onto it, counting to three and releasing the air through pursed lips. The hiss is that of a serpent writhing in the pit of doubt.

Eyes closed and welcoming the restraint the darkness brings, I fight to maintain reason. It is the first time for as long as I can remember that I have been close to well and truly losing my shit. Even though I want to stay here, safe and secure, there is no real choice. I'm a pariah, unwelcome because of the dangers I bring to my young host.

Even if I were to ask her to forgo a quest to a place where she will not feel welcome, and go with me to Crowley's farm, I still pose too much of a risk. The Samaritans will never stop looking and one day they could get lucky. I get it—understand it—but the very thought of being alone out there in the deranged realm beyond the door of this house threatens to penetrate the brittle shield of faux strength behind which I now hide.

Now there are the tears—of anger, of frustration, of self-pity. But most of all, they are there because I'm fucking scared. I'm locked into a design of no choice and there's no escaping it. Yet I must do what is right, what I would want someone to do for Poppy if they had put her in the same position.

I grab my bag from where Shelly has left it on the kitchen floor and heave it to the front door. On the threshold I make the decision that, in order to survive, I must stick to what I know and that, as much as it feels like the greatest backward step taken by a man, is Crowley's farm. I will double back, certain that in a day's time I will be back on familiar ground, my future uncertain but safe.

Well, safer than here, at least.

With a small groan of misery, I open the door and step outside; my fate now in the hands of my own ineptitude.

CHAPTER TWELVE

On my way up the path to the front gate, I see the dead Rottweiler. It is lying on its side, its head at a right-angle to the hedge. I notice the eye socket I gouged has been replaced by a ball bearing, making the beast look like a hideous canine-machine hybrid. Shelly is a damn good shot.

I open and close the gate, reaching over to shove the latch back in place. And now I'm creeping across the urban scene. The sky has become milky grey and there is a cool breeze upon my face. The air smells of rain and every footfall is painfully loud. Eyes flitting from building to building, I leave Shelly and her haven behind, wondering where she is, wondering if she is watching me now from her hideaway. I also think about Paul, hoping beyond hope I don't stumble upon his torn, ravaged body.

What I don't expect is to see a figure emerging from the garden hedge fifty yards ahead. It is facing away from me and I stall; a stab of dread in my chest. The figure is tall, and, despite the heavy coat, I can see a thin frame. There is also a rucksack on one shoulder and as it turns to face me, a rifle clasped in both hands.

Anxiety falls away as my mind registers the fedora.

"Paul!" The cry is out of my mouth before I have time to register caution.

"Stay back!" he cries. "Samaritans!"

I ignore his warnings and hobble towards him. This man is somehow alive and therefore so is our quest. As I draw closer, I can see two things instantly. The first is the wild look in his eyes. The second is the blood. It streaks his hands and the sleeves of his coat, glistening like dawn dew.

"Thank Christ you're okay. What's happened?"

He shakes his head, holding up his blood-streaked hands. "It's not mine."

I give him my 'can you expand on that' face.

"Fucking dog's blood, Chris. What else?"

What else, indeed? I'm feeling jittery, the effects of too much adrenaline over too short a time.

I calm myself by asking a question. "You see a girl out here? A teenager, she's deaf."

Alarm leaves its mark on Paul's face. "Deaf? You mean, she's a Harbinger?"

I feel irritation bristle through me. "That's a Samaritan word. Her name's Shelly and she saved my life last night."

"Thought I did that?"

This is the second time in twelve hours someone has staked a claim on my mortality. The irony scuppers my annoyance. "You see her?"

"No," he says. "But even if I had there isn't no way I'm going near her. She'll attract Samaritans like a picnic attracts fucking wasps."

I brush past him. "I don't care, Paul. I don't *fucking* care!"

I'm moving again, faster (or at least as fast as I can go). Paul is at my shoulder, muttering, but I sense his resignation at my decision to head out of the estate and onto the main road. As we approach the junction, we slow and hunker down behind a tangled privet.

I peer out, the scent of wet hedgerows in my nostrils. When I see the scene to our right, my hands go to my mouth to stifle a cry of horror.

***

Shelly hangs from an acacia fifty yards away. Her hands are bound behind her back, and her throat has been slit. Blood has drained down her blouse and onto her jeans, her head is slumped forward, face mercifully hidden from view.

My voice is like glass, fragile and broken. "Oh, Christ. This is my fault, my fault."

"It's nobody's fault but those fuckers masquerading as human beings," Paul says softly. "And we'll be getting dragged into this, too, if we don't get the hell out of here."

My eyes can't pull away from the girl in the tree. I want to take the image in, I want to own it so that I can savour the guilt it will bring later, when I'm alone and atoning for driving her out of her own home and into the arms of monsters.

Paul is still talking, though it comes to me as though through plate glass.

"We go left, stick to the verges until we clear the town. Who knows, we might get lucky."

"Lucky?" I can hear the contempt in my voice. "Is that what this is?"

Paul's face is next to mine, his eyes flair with anger. "Damn right it is. You want to go back to being a slave, Chris? Or would you prefer to join her in a fucking tree? If those choices don't suit then yeah, we're going to need a heavy dose of luck to make it."

I chew my lip rather than make any kind of retort. He's right but I can't buy into this right now. I'd rather curl up into a ball and forget everything. I'm a child in this hateful new world.

Paul isn't having any of it; he grabs me and yanks me to my feet before I have time to protest. "Luck or judgement, we're going. Right NOW!"

I am a passenger, a stooge, and allow him to pull me along as my mind falters with the horror of what has happened, what *is* happening. There comes a sound that adds to the ambience, an engine rumbling from behind us, further up the ~~man~~ road.

"Shit," Paul breathes. "The bastards are still here."

Rage surges through me, my thoughts are irrational, I want to run down the road and beat the living shit out of the first Samaritan that jumps out of the flatbed, not caring if I get caught and serve as a slave for a lifetime; reprisal will be my reward.

But, as always, Paul injects reason into the madness. "I can see you're hurting. But this isn't a fight either of us can win. We can only stay alive and remember these times when we get to pay these fuckers back."

As a speech it's tired and worn, but it does the job, tapping into my desire—perhaps selfishly—to stay alive and get out of here.

We use the overgrown gardens and hedgerows as allies, blending in, becoming invisible to the squad of Samaritans as they cruise the main street.

In places we climb fences smothered in creeping ivy and bracken, leaving hands and arms covered in more scratches than we already have; or we scale sheds and playhouses of families long since silenced, long since dead. Our mission is freedom and, like swords sworn to kings, we are loyal to the cause.

I look right and see twin patio doors of plastic and glass. Pressing against the panes is a shape, human in form. At first, I think it is an unfortunate, who has died and become one with the door, but then it moves, and the squeak of plastic frame and the crack of window glass tell me that we're in real fucking trouble.

CHAPTER THIRTEEN

The frame gives out before the reinforced glass. The doors explode outwards, catching unawares the big man pummelling them, the momentum dumping him onto the overgrown lawns. He scrambles to his feet, bringing a handgun up with him as he comes to his knees. I also see that the barrel is aimed at me like an unblinking, black eye.

Before I know what's happening, I am shoved aside and I go sprawling into the wet grass, rolling several times, my knee painfully straining against Crowley's Gift, my arm joining in along the way. Moaning in pain, I hear the gunshot and, despite instincts to stay supine, sit up to find the Samaritan staggering backwards, towards the doors he's been determined to put through in the need to get to us.

His trench coat flaps like the wings of a great bat, his *Tell-Pad* is shattered and sparking, and a bloody smear is splashed across his breast. Falling backwards, the Samaritan smashes into the patio doors where he slumps to the floor.

Standing amongst the grass is Paul; rifle held at hip-height, face grim. As I get to my feet, he stares at me and for one, horrifying second I don't see any recognition in his gaze. Then his face softens and there is only sadness in his voice.

"Didn't want to have to do that," he says. "But it's done and now we have to finish it."

"Meaning what?"

"We've taken one of theirs, they'll want blood. They'll never stop."

Given that Paul had pulled the trigger, I wanted to point out that in terms of responsibility 'we've taken one of theirs' wasn't exactly accurate. I decide to keep my mouth shut and wait for clarification on what is expected of me.

"Know about guns?"

"I think we've already established that one."

Paul goes over to the prostrate Samaritan and retrieves his weapon. He promptly hands to me. I look at it as though it is an alien artefact.

"Take it."

Hesitant, I reach for the gun and an impatient Paul shoves it against my palm. The metal is cold to the touch and has an odd, greasy layer that has me gripping it tight for fear of dropping it.

"What do I do?"

"Get as close as you can and aim for the body. Don't yank on the trigger, squeeze it gently. It's a Glock and it'll kick some."

"Anything else?"

"Yeah. Try not to shoot either of us."

I gulp, hard. Like stale coffee, reality is a difficult to swallow.

***

We're inside the house from which the Samaritan broke free, before Paul shot him like a mad dog, leaving him to bleed out on the patio.

Paul presses his back against the lounge wall, listening out for any sounds coming from deep inside the house. "Samaritans are using the properties to head us off. We have the advantage because we can hear them a mile off."

"You'd think they'd bring someone who can hear with them. You know, to even the odds?"

"You kidding?" Paul scoffs. "It'd be like taking your Lamborghini and parking it in the middle of Nechells and expecting it to still be there when you get back."

I know what he is getting at, but I still feel uncomfortable with council estate stereotyping. I feel even more disconcerted by the thought of sneaking up on someone and shooting them point-blank. Part of me has a whimsical hope that the Samaritans will decide to give up their search and we can sidle away come nightfall.

In his wisdom, Paul insists we must, "Take the fight to them", and I can only think that he's got far more faith in my abilities with a gun than I have. Either that or he really has lost his mind and wants to go out swinging.

"They'll have a dog with them, right?"

Paul nods. "We'll have to take it out, too."

"Maybe they'll get spooked by that and retreat?" I'm a little embarrassed by just how much I'm pinning on this fantasy. Paul brings me down to earth a few seconds later.

"These guys aren't going to stop, Chris." He talks slowly, like I'm stupid. "Yeah, they might startle and get the hell out of here, but they'll be back tomorrow with more hounds and more people. And they'll hunt us down."

I look at the gun hanging limply in my hands, feeling more pathetic than ever.

"Great."

We make our way into the next room, the lounge giving way to a dining area with a dusty beech wood table. There's a bloody smear on the wall where a palm and splayed fingers have been pressed against the wallpaper. But it is so old the handprint is the colour of tar. One of the chairs is tipped over and there's a moth-eaten teddy bear splashed with more black spots lying underneath the table legs.

An image of the final meal with Evie and Poppy begins to make itself known, but I'm somehow able to quash it with thoughts of having my brains blown out by an irate sociopath in a trench coat.

Paul moves to the doorway and I dutifully follow, the Glock aimed at the carpet to make sure I don't absently discharge it into his unsuspecting spine.

No, Chris, we're only shooting the bad guys in the back today. My mind is a joker even at the most solemn of times. Whatever happened to the era when the biggest danger in my day was a classroom full of bored 7-year-old kids grasping Magic Markers?

The compulsive urge to giggle is now an enemy of focus. My free hand comes up to my mouth and I try to suffocate any evidence of mirth. It crosses my mind that madness is trying to assert itself and this throws water on my escalating emotions.

We are in the entrance hall and the front door is thrown wide, the jamb surrounding the locking mechanism is splintered from where the dead Samaritan has gained brutish entry.

The guttural grunts and snorts come soon after, Paul taking a step back as an approaching newcomer from the path outside throws an oily shadow on the welcome mat by the front door.

The Beagle appears seconds later, unable to bark, it emits pitiful rasps, saliva and snot spraying the walls and carpets as it crosses the doorstep and into the hall. The leash about its neck becomes a diagonal slash on the air as it yanks its owner with it.

The Samaritan who lumbers through the doorway is big, the trench coat making them almost shapeless. They are just as surprised as we all stare at each other, the moment given cadence via the dog's rasps and warbling growl.

The man in the trench coat has a smoky, grey beard, thick and sculpted into a monolith at his chin. Blue eyes seem to have a mix of surprise, anger and deep, deep fear. The kind of fear that makes men do bad things to good people.

His *Tell-Pad* is blank but the lamp on his shoulder is winking furiously as his unseen colleague tries to communicate with him.

Then, many things seem to happen at once.

In the flurry of movement that follows, the Samaritan lifts his other hand and the gun he holds is not dissimilar to mine, though I figure he's a damn-sight more proficient.

"Shoot the fucker!" Paul yells, and I aim the Glock at the hulking figure in the doorway as Paul uses his rifle to put down the dog, effectively, efficiently and without hesitation.

The rifle shot is loud, and so—too—is the cry from the Samaritan as he watches his only connection to the hearing world slump to the carpet, the hind legs spasming for a few seconds before lying still, forever.

My gun aims at his chest but my hands tremble so badly the muzzle zig-zags in the air. In my mind I am screaming *this is a person, this is a person*, and I am mesmerised by the words as they ricochet through my brain.

Hesitancy costs seconds and the Samaritan takes aim at my head, then there is another gunshot and I watch the guy's *Tell-Pad* shatter and blood pumps from his chest. He staggers backwards through the front door. For a second, his hand, still holding onto the leash, drags his poor, dead dog with him.

"For fuck's sake, Chris!" Paul is having trouble hiding his frustration with my lack of action. "Get your act together, man!"

More shots can be heard from outside and the hallway is riddled with tiny explosions. They tear into the wood of the banister and punch holes in the terrible wallpaper. A picture of a boat on a lake gets shredded and tumbles to the carpet, the glass shatters and arcs through the air like droplets of water has escaped from the painting.

We both scramble for cover and hear the running of feet as someone comes up the path leading to the house. The rifle in Paul's hands makes a thick clicking noise as he tries to return fire.

"Damn it!" he cries before jumping into the room opposite the stairs, where he lands heavily with an 'oof' sound. More bullets follow, more chunks of plaster are torn from the walls.

I tumble backwards and see the shape of another Samaritan coming through the doorway. This time I grasp my wrist to steady the aim, grimacing against the pain of my forearm, yet still shooting before I can even think of not doing so.

There follows so many shots I'm not sure what's happening, the gun bucking in my hands, the doorframe taking a few rounds but I'm so close it's nearly impossible to not hit the Samaritan stumbling into the hall.

The cry is short, sharp and the body hits the open door before pin wheeling into the banister and crashing onto the stairs. There is a heavy gasping sound and I realise it is coming from the person I have just shot.

On all fours I crawl towards the doorway, my disabled leg trails along behind me. Taking a tentative peek outside I can see there is a flatbed truck parked at the front of the house on the main street.

Nothing moves, the eerie silence after the chaos of the past few minutes leaves me off kilter. I stand and, to my right, Paul comes gingerly from his hiding place.

"See anything?"

"Just their truck."

"We got the three of 'em."

The heavy breathing continues behind us and I turn to the Samaritan I've blasted and who now is lying supine on the stairs. Paul joins me as we look down at the boy gasping for air. Where the bullet has struck his neck, bubbles fizz as though he has a strawberry soda pouring through the wound.

"Can't be older than sixteen," I whisper. "What have I done?"

The weapon in my hand drops to the floor, a statement of my contempt for what I've become, what I *am*.

Kid-killer.

"*What you've done* is stay alive and that's all we have now."

Paul steps up to the boy and places the muzzle of the rifle against his brow. There is no acknowledgement in the kid's eyes, just the faraway look of the dying.

The rifle quickens the boy's passing with a report that is as loud as any I have heard in the past half an hour. It is an act of mercy and an execution blended together until it becomes one and the same.

Paul turns to me, his face grim. "We'll drag them all out into the street. I guess the dogs will be eating well for the next few days."

"Don't you think we should hide the bodies?

In thought, Paul taps a finger to his lips, then nods. "Seems you're adapting to life out here after all."

I bow my head, not seeing anything good in his statement.

CHAPTER FOURTEEN

The woods are a relief after the claustrophobic constraints of the estate. We have walked for three hours straight, putting as much distance as possible between us and the carnage we have left piled in the loft of the house with bloodstained-handprint wallpaper.

The flatbed has been driven into a barn on the edge of town. Now it is keeping company with rusting farm equipment and the voles who riddle the hay bales.

My first thought had been to use the flatbed. It would have meant my ankle and knee not hurting like hell as it does now. I'm munching on painkillers; the bitter taste reflects my current outlook. Paul put things into perspective when I'd suggested commandeering the truck.

"If you want to make it that easy for Samaritans to find us, how about we get in and drive it all the way back to Cathedral?"

That had ended the discussion, decision well and truly made. Since that point, Paul has said very little, carrying with him an air of disdain. I'm guessing he's not quite finished being pissed at me for how I responded with the gun. Or, more appropriately: how I *didn't* use the gun. Be that as it may, three people are still dead, one of them a teen. I console myself with the thought that they were all responsible for Shelly's death, the irony that I am equally complicit is not lost on me.

That we're still alive and free makes the disquiet I feel no less potent.

No less ashamed.

***

"Want a hotdog?"

Paul waves the tinned frankfurters under my nose. The can has sat in the campfire and the sausages have boiled in their own brine. The chef protects his hand from the heat with a grubby swatch of denim.

I jab my fork into the brine and receive two sausages.

"Thanks."

"You're welcome."

Paul's mood has lifted somewhat since we set up camp. Perhaps he's come to terms with my ineptitude; he's insisted I bring the Glock along, handing it back to me before we left the estate. I'd tried to leave it in the hallway. Now it's in the waistband of my trousers and I feel like some witless survivalist.

I blow on my food and take a bite. Though I don't feel hungry, the salty taste of the frankfurters has me salivating and I'm suddenly ravenous, wolfing down the rest in mere seconds.

"That's the most life I've seen in you for three days," Paul laughs. The flickering firelight makes his face oscillate between deep, cavernous creases and blanched moonscape, evil and the divine winking in and out like a theological beacon.

The smile on my lips is genuine but Paul's assessment is way off. I've never felt more animated, more alive, than after the shootout in the hallway. I've come close to death and I didn't want it, not then and certainly not now. Perhaps I'm a coward, perhaps it's instinct to want to stay in this shit-show of a world, no matter what stain it puts upon my soul.

There is a rustling sound as Paul searches inside the bag at his side. From it he pulls his radio and clicks it into life. The familiar static adds to the crackles from the campfire.

"Let's see if we can inject a little bit of good nature into the proceedings," Paul says as he twiddles the dial. "Never helps that the frequency changes like the weather."

"Maybe it is protection," I offer. "To stop people locating them?"

"You could be right. Still, it's a pain in the arse. Hide and seek in the ether."

The static gives way to undulating whistles indicating an open channel. Then we hear it, the voice of the angel of the airwaves. She talks about liberty and a world free from horror. Somehow, out here in the very place from which we experience such terrible happenings, her words are more potent than ever.

As I ruminate, Paul gets out his map and tilts it so that he can see the contour lines. "Co-ordinates put her ten miles south-east but—"

"But what?"

He taps the map with an index finger. "There's a damn town in the way. 'Davenport', it says here."

I sigh. "Crowley spoke of it once. Told me the place was occupied by deaf people, those lost to MNG-U. It was on his 'no-go' list."

"What list was that?" Paul quizzes.

"Places we could not go to together. He was worried he'd lose me to the villagers."

"Looks like the fever left him with some brains."

"Can't we skirt it?"

Paul mulls this over. "Take us too far out of our way. I'm no doctor, but I'm guessing you're struggling with that knee of yours as it is."

He is right. The going has been arduous on my leg, despite my diet of painkillers. I push back regardless. "We had a deal. You can press on, I got my radio, and I've got a map. And I sure as hell have got the incentive to follow on behind."

Paul's face softens. "I know that, and I don't doubt it. But words are one thing. Leaving another man behind for real isn't as easy."

Silence hangs around for a while. Paul uses the gap to take a swig from his canteen.

"There's always a chance Crowley was talking bullshit," I suggest. "He was as paranoid as they come. The place might be empty."

Paul clips the canteen onto the webbing of his rucksack. "Anything is possible. But not everyone migrated back to the cities. Sometimes the need to be near home is more powerful than the need to be safe. One and the same thing to many, I'd say."

"What about you, Paul? Do you feel safe?"

His eyes meet mine, his face fixed, stern. "That's not the way to think out here. All it does is make you hesitant. Then it makes you ineffective. You may as well lie down and wait for the end to come."

"Okay."

The terms of reference for staying alive had changed and I am playing catch up, big time. Perhaps it is time to get with the programme and step up to the challenges I have chosen to embrace when I decided to follow the lure of the voice on the radio.

Paul puts a hand inside his coat and retrieves a photograph. He hands it to me and, for reasons I cannot explain, I'm initially hesitant to take it. Maybe it is because photographs usually represent precious moments in time, or people held dear, and now they only represent what has been taken from us all, becoming items to mock and provoke endless mourning.

The photograph is dog eared and smudged. It depicts a woman—I estimate is in her forties—her black hair highlighted with the first steaks of grey. She has a warm smile and eyes that are dark pools, just like the man who has handed me the photograph.

"Becky," he says by way of explanation. "Daughters, eh? What is it a father wouldn't do for his little girl?"

I understood this all too well, of course. Fathers would do anything, but the fever is way beyond this injunction.

He takes the photograph when I hand it back, stowing it into his coat pocket once more. Paul lets out a soft sigh, and I recognise it for what it is: love, deep and unconditional. I don't have the heart to ask if she is dead or deaf.

I feel his eyes on me. I look up and he has made no attempt to unlock his gaze. "So?'

"Huh?"

He rests his hands in his lap. "We going to carry on as planned, or what?"

"You got a plan?"

"Yeah. And it's so obvious, even *you* would come up with it at some point."

Like rats, backhanded compliments can also survive the apocalypse.

CHAPTER FIFTEEN

We have moved on and the night is giving way to a new day. The air is alive with birdsong and the light has an ethereal quality, indicating that we are in for at least some sunshine. After travelling by night for a while, it seems odd now to be walking in daylight. It's true that I feel way too vulnerable, but part of me is enjoying this time spent in broad daylight.

It is also a means to an end, our progression through Davenport depends on it.

Paul stops in the middle of the road we are now following. He pulls the weathered map from his rucksack, and peers at it thoughtfully, his mouth moving in a slow rhythm as he chews on a piece of bacon jerky that he's found in his coat pocket.

As he considers the map, I sense his reticence. "What is it?"

He leans towards me and points at a line on the map. "This road is taking us straight to Davenport. Once we get around the next bend, we'll be in sight and there's no turning back."

"We have *the* plan, right?"

"Of course."

The Plan is more a reckless and dangerous bluff. We are going into Davenport pretending we are deafened by MNG-U, and then blag our way through until we get beyond their borders.

As a concept it seems flimsy but it's the only real chance we have of cleaving twenty miles off our journey to the Promised Land. The risks are, of course, significant but then again so is the prize: safety, security, the chance to start again in a world free of Samaritans and crazed survivors of the plague.

"Let's just be careful, okay?" I say. "No heroics."

Paul smiles and his eyes are alive with mischief. I'm not sure if this is a good thing or not. "You have it, Chris."

With a deep breath, we press on.

***

The village of Davenport appears as we turn a slow and steady bend in the road. By this time, poplars line both sides and mask the smattering of white cottages until the very last moment. I can see thatched roofs as grey as thunderheads nestling in a crease of the green countryside below.

Paul stops and hunkers down, pulling a small pair of field glasses from the folds of his coat. He scans the way ahead and grunts.

"What you see?"

He offers me the glasses. "Take a look."

I hold the eyepieces to my sockets, adjusting the rangefinder to sharpen the focus. The image shudders in my inexperienced hands, yet I can see Davenport clearly enough.

There is a corrugated, metal barrier annexing the village from the rest of the world. Ramparts on the other side of the structure are made plain by the several figures looking out upon the road. On occasion I see crude hand gestures—localised sign language—as the guards communicate with each other, others have *Tell-Pad*s. These confirm our suspicions; this is a place for those who have fallen victim of MNG-U.

Below the barrier there is movement. The edge of a long, squat rectangle appears as a gate is drawn to the left and a cluster of people come through. At first, I have difficulty making out what the hell is happening. The group is moving in an odd way—shuffling—and I adjust the viewfinder to gain greater clarity.

I see four people, standing back to back; arms linked at the elbows, three men, one woman, each with a handgun.

They shuffle along, the concentration pulling their faces into tight frowns.

"What the hell?" I whisper.

Paul's voice comes to me. "What you're looking at is fear. This is what they've become, lost and fragile. We replace their vulnerability, give them a little hope."

I continue to follow the group as they move, crab-like down the road, towards us. The sight is both saddening and pathetic. I think of Crowley and his endless rambling nights of drinking hooch, mourning his hearing, and to my surprise find myself overcome with a profound sense of sadness. Not just for him, but for all of us, deaf and hearing, and what fate has made of us all.

I watch and my companion continues to speak, voice low and solemn. It sounds like a eulogy for the damned, and not once feels out of place.

"Even with everything we've lost, we hearing folk got the better deal in the end. I came to that conclusion some time ago."

I consider Crowley's Gift and a vein of anger coursed through me. "I'm not so sure. Experience is relative, isn't it?" I turn to face him, and that is when I see the butt of his rifle coming towards my head.

There is a moment of sickening pain, before fireflies dance in the sudden, complete darkness.

**

I come to on a cot, my head a throbbing entity. My hands go to my brow where fingers feel a smooth lump the size of a goose egg, and I am reminded of the time I knocked myself out so I could spend some time with the radio. This thought opens floodgates and other memories pour into my brain as I wince at the fiery flashes of pain my probing fingers elicit from the wound site. If my head gets any more knocks, I fear it will become square.

"Shit."

I slowly become aware of my surroundings, if not of my predicament. The room I'm in is basic, emerging from a hazy fog as my senses return to some semblance of normalcy.

Though rudimentary, the room is spacious and well decorated. Aside from my bed, there's an *Ikea* table of thin, blanched wood and metal legs, and a mirror stuck on the far wall reflects my shaky, recovering image. The window to my left allows light to settle upon the room and its contents. There is a small fridge and a sink unit, a kettle and tea making facilities. I can see the white tiles of a wet room through an open door to the right. In all, it has the feel and appearance, even down to the plain, magnolia paintwork, of a low-budget hotel room.

My sight slowly returns; the fuzzy edges of the table and white goods sharpen. The dull throb in my skull remains a constant reminder of the blow at the hands of Paul and the butt of his rifle.

I stand and wait for the apartment to stop shimmying before my eyes, swallow hard against the surge of nausea in my gut. I lean against the wall, using it as both crutch and guide, as I head to the door I assume is the exit.

Regaining balance, I navigate the doorframe that marks the wet room, risking a peek inside, taking in the usual paraphernalia, soap, an electric toothbrush on its charger; plump blue towels that are neatly folded on a counter to the left of a pristine shaving mirror. Seems hygiene is held in higher esteem than trust these days. I curb my bitterness, finding its injunction hard to stomach.

I figure the exit will be locked even as I make to grasp the brass handle. I pump the lever a few times regardless, the door rattling in its frame as I fruitlessly push and pull.

Through the headache, questions vie for attention, yet no sooner has notion and confusion declared war on each other, the muted sounds of cheering come to me.

Stronger now, fuelled by anxiety and curiosity, I make for the window, and look out through horizontal slats. The people of Davenport are in a circle in the street below. To my horror I can see there are others with them.

There are several people—men, women, a few children—sitting in wheelchairs, blankets over their laps.

The faces of these people are blank with abject misery. I recognise the trait as I have seen it so often in the mirror of my room at Crowley's farm, and again just now in my new cell.

I see one of the seated wretches—a man with black hair—look over to a young boy no older than 9 years old, his lips move and the boy turns his head only to be cuffed about the face by the woman standing next to his chair. The woman makes more gestures at the boy who is now crying, and I hear the thick voice of the deafened woman as she chastises him.

The man with black hair is next to receive the wrath of the woman, who now strides over to him and punches him in the sternum without breaking stride. The man cries out and his blanket slips from his lap and to the floor. I watch in horror when I see his legs are mere stumps that flail up and down as he deals with the pain. My eyes go to all those in the wheelchairs, each with their covers, and I fear the worse.

The woman scoops up the blanket and throws it at the man who proceeds to cover his ruined legs as he sobs in despair.

The crowd watch all of this and show their approval at this bizarre, brutal kind of discipline. The sounds they make are thick and gruff, a bizarre caricature of a cheer.

Before I'm overcome by disgust, two people enter the square. I recognise one faster than the other. They are suddenly the focus of the crowd's accolades; hands wave and the strange ululations fill the air.

Paul stands, stoic and smiling, his hands gesticulating as he accepts the reverence from the crowd. In this moment I realise I can hate someone more than Crowley. Paul has earned the top spot with total ease. Had he been in the room with me, I fear I would find the will to kill him as easy as swatting a fly. I'm guessing Paul knows it too, that's maybe why I'm locked in here.

The thought is a fleeting ghost as I see the second person. It takes a few seconds, but I recognised her as the woman from Paul's photograph.

Becky, his daughter.

CHAPTER SIXTEEN

The door handle clatters and keys click into the lock. After a few seconds of shimmying, the door swings inwards and Paul is standing in the doorway, the Glock pointing at me.

"Say you're not going to do anything stupid?"

"I can't think of anything I can do more stupid than ever trusting you. I'm guessing your name isn't even Paul."

"You're right, it's Francis. And don't be like that, Chris." He walks into the room and jabs the gun in the direction of the armchair.

"Like what? Wanting for the first time in my life to seriously fuck someone up?"

"The Dwayne Johnson shit just isn't you."

"No one is as they seem these days. Can you take the chance?"

"Yes. Sit down."

This time it's an order, the tone: sedate, yet firm. And it's backed up by the gun. I shuffle to the chair and slump back into it. I protest by giving my captor a heated stare that has no impact at all.

"Why are you here?"

"I figure you'd need an explanation."

"About what? Why you turned those poor bastards outside into paraplegics?"

He gestures to Crowley's Gift. "We all have different ways of protecting our investments."

"They're fucking *people*."

"More than that, Chris. Those good souls out there are the difference between life and death. They are gods. And they're coveted as such. Well fed, well housed, and tended to by those who they serve. In their own way they are loved. They are home."

I recall the earlier assault on the child and the man with black hair.

"Unless they don't do as they're told."

He merely shrugs. "Discipline has always been part of family life. Why should it be any different today? Without it there are no ground rules. And without rules you get chaos."

"If this is The Refuge it sure as hell doesn't sound like the fucking spot ads."

Again, he shrugs. "It's carrot and sticks these days. You have to cast a wide net. But sometimes you get lucky, sometimes people come to you."

His comment is loaded, and I'm meant to work it out. The conclusion comes quickly, the anger stoking my mind, driving it.

"Crowley?"

"Crowley," he confirms. "He came here three times by all accounts. To barter and trade. I was always out there, you see, looking for people like us. But I was here on his last visit. You could smell the fear, the apprehension when he saw me. It's like he knew I saw through him, knew his *little secret*, and he got out of here like his arse was alight. Didn't take much to follow him to his place and see what a treasure he was hiding."

He sniggers at the memory.

I consider the irony that Crowley's single-mindedness is still more alive than he is, taunting me from the beyond. Maybe he does have a right to smirk.

"And the broadcasts over the radio, the woman? All bullshit?"

"Aye, but they served their purpose. The woman, well that's one of the folks out there, working on the promise of keeping her hands as long as she just keeps on talking."

"You're a great employer."

He smiles and it is cold. "I'm the only one in town. There's no point getting pissed at me. You wanted to leave Crowley, I gave you incentive and opportunity, and you fucking took them both."

"That's not a choice."

"Oh, come on, Chris! You seriously think you just happened across a perfectly functioning wireless radio? Don't be so fucking *naive*. I put it there, bait on the hook. And you bit, my friend, and you never let go. You had choices; don't you say otherwise."

His logic is skewed; he's duped me but has no insight. I learned a long time ago not to challenge the deluded. I wonder if I toe the line, my legs can stay attached to my body.

My macabre thoughts are interrupted by a shuffling sound from the doorway. There is a landing outside; the staves of a staircase aptly look like bars of a prison. Beyond the doorframe, a shadow is on the carpet; a person hiding out of sight yet betrayed by the light behind them.

A sneeze comes seconds later.

He gives a warm grin before responding to the disembodied sound by stomping his foot three times.

In response, Becky emerges. I recognise her black-grey hair immediately. She scuttles into the room and stands behind her father, peering out from over his shoulder, hiding like a toddler. It is an action that Poppy used whenever in the company of strangers. The memory warms my heart before breaking it.

Despite the disgust at my predicament, I raise my hand in a token wave.

Becky looks at me with her dark eyes and waves back, the movement is uncertain.

I return her gesture with a smile. It's not her fault the world is as fucked as it is, after all.

She steps out and to stand beside her father. Close up, Becky is a delicate thing, some would say sickly. Her movement is childlike, and I suspect there is some cognitive impairment in her. Whether this is down to MNG-U or something from before all this bedlam, I'm not sure.

My attention is soon elsewhere as her small frame is covered in a cheese-cloth dress of yellow and white gingham. The pattern plays with my eyes and it is a few seconds before I see what hangs from her neck.

The small delicate effigy of a dolphin, suspended from shoelace, a necklace.

Shelly's necklace.

My smile slips and a small groan emerges from the back of my throat. Hands gripping the arms of the chair, I try to rationalise why the very necklace Shelly told me her mother gave for her tenth birthday has ended up around the neck of Francis' daughter.

To save time I point to it. "That's nice. Where you get it?"

Becky can't hear me, but she gets it. Without hesitation, she points at her father. Her chest swells with pride.

My eyes go to Francis. He has altered his position slightly, one foot forward as though bracing for assault.

"You?"

"Yes. Me."

"Why?"

"It's the law. The world is to be purged of Harbingers, remember?"

"What happened to it being bullshit for people who need a scapegoat?"

He smiles as I quote his words. "When you got a fish on the hook, you'll do whatever to land them. Harbingers brought our world to an end, Chris. My Becky has been defiled by their obscenity; her mother didn't even make it this far. Harbingers are responsible for that; I have no doubt. You want to believe otherwise then that's your call. But I did my duty, and I'll not lose any sleep over it."

The emotions running through me are a fusion, of anger and rage, of despair and, of course, guilt. It is culpability that colours what happens next, the tears flow and hands that want to claw around Francis' neck and choke the life from his heinous soul instead wrap around me, and I slowly rock in the seat, as though the self-comfort will ease the fact that I am just as responsible for Shelly's death as the monster across the room.

It almost works, but delusion has become as much a tool for survival as a Glock.

Like so many these days, I have learned this the hard way. Yet this latest shock is different, this time there is no mutated virus, no Samaritans and no Crowley. The fate of Shelly is mine to own, a yoke that I shall carry for as long as the moments I have left on the Earth.

CHAPTER SEVENTEEN

I am assured by Francis that, if I fulfil my duties to Becky, no harm will come to me. That I bow to the wiles of slavery is testament to the man I have probably always been, a coward with too much to say. These days, it's a relief that there aren't too many around able to hear my self-deception.

It's just me and my tarnished conscience.

From my room window, I look down upon the town of Davenport, the people going about their business, pushing their maimed, hearing slaves around as though taking a dear relative out for some fresh air. There are children running around with arms outstretched, pretending to be aeroplanes, kicking a football about the town square, being chased away when the ball hits a window or passer-by.

The whole thing reeks of normality, but it isn't. It is a twisted parody, life bent out of shape, rebranded for a new social order, a new kind of family.

Francis' voice comes to me. *"What is it a father wouldn't do for his little girl?"*

Nothing, it would seem. The incentive for deception is there in all its glory.

Abduction, mutilation and murder are tools to keep his people—his daughter—safe.

And me? Well, it appears that I am another tool for his toolbox.

I feel the weight of it, the responsibility, endless days being the ears for a multitude in times of ever-present danger. It has me reeling, away from the window, eyes blurred, not from fugue but tears of grief as I clutch at the doorframe to the bathroom, gasping for air.

I don't want such a charge! It's been bad enough taking the weight for Crowley. Now it will be expected of an entire town, servitude without end. The realisation is perhaps made more potent by my brief taste of freedom, this is unclear.

There is one certainty, it has made the thought to end any prospect of returning to service so much easier.

I step into the bathroom and snatch the electric toothbrush from its cradle in one smooth action. I remove the head and cast it aside, exposing the stainless-steel shaft. Activating the device, the barrel numbing the palm of my hand, I watch, mesmerised as the slim steel strip oscillates.

There is no doubt I am a coward, and it is this part of me that asks now what will become of the man I leave behind. Perhaps in his rage, Francis will put a bullet in my head, do the good deed that I cannot. Perhaps he will take my hands and legs anyway, just for the hell of it, payback for thwarting his attempts to provide safety and security for his precious daughter, this damned town.

For a few seconds I listen to the buzz in the air, and in the mirror give myself a wan smile when I recognised that the angry, incessant hum from the toothbrush is going to be the last sound I will ever hear.

Without pause, I ram the head of the toothbrush into my left ear, agony flares in my cheek and shoots down my neck. Blood and tears flow as the pain bends me double.

But with my groans comes something else. Laughter, a harsh cackle as I feel I now have the chance to avenge Shelly, and not just avenge her, but atone for my part in her demise.

My right ear is now a wall of dead air, my neck and shoulder, wet with blood. Still laughing, still weeping, I swap hands and bring the toothbrush up again.

The sense of joy consumes like fire as I find peace in silence.

BIOGRAPHY

Dave Jeffery is the author of 14 novels, two collections, and numerous short stories. His "Necropolis Rising" series and yeti adventure *Frostbite* have both featured on the Amazon #1 bestseller list. His YA work features critically acclaimed "Beatrice Beecham" supernatural mystery series and *Finding Jericho*, a contemporary mental health novel that was featured on the BBC Health and the Independent Schools Entrance Examination Board's recommended reading lists.

Dave is a member of the Society of Authors, British Fantasy Society (where he is a regular book reviewer), and the Horror Writers Association. He is also a registered mental health professional with a BSc (Hons) in Mental Health Studies and a Master of Science Degree in Health Studies.

Dave Jeffery is married with two children and lives in Worcestershire, UK.

More about him can be found at:

https://davejeffery.webs.com/

ADRIAN BALDWIN (COVER ARTIST)

Adrian is a Mancunian now living and working in Wales. Back in the 1990s, he wrote for various TV shows/personalities: Smith & Jones, Clive Anderson, Brian Conley, Paul McKenna, Hale & Pace, Rory Bremner (and a few others). Wooo, get him! Since then, he has written three screenplays—one of which received generous financial backing from the Film Agency for Wales. Then along came the global recession which kicked the UK Film industry in the nuts. What a bummer! Not to be outdone, he turned to novel writing—which had always been his real dream—and, in particular, a genre he feels is often overlooked; a genre he has always been a fan of: Dark Comedy (sometimes referred to as Horror's weird cousin). *Barnacle Brat* (a dark comedy for grown-ups), his first novel won Indie Novel of the Year 2016 award; his second novel *Stanley Mccloud Must Die!* (more dark comedy for grown-ups) published in 2016 and his third: *The Snowman And The Scarecrow* (another dark comedy for grown-ups) published in 2018. Adrian Baldwin has also written and published a number of dark comedy short stories. He designs book covers too—not just for his own books but for a growing number of publishers. For more information on the award-winning author, check out: https://adrianbaldwin.info/

DEMAIN PUBLISHING

To keep up to-date on all news DEMAIN (including future submission calls and releases) you can follow us in a number of ways:

BLOG:
www.demainpublishingblog.weebly.com

TWITTER:
@DemainPubUk

FACEBOOK PAGE:
Demain Publishing

INSTAGRAM:
demainpublishing

Printed in Great Britain
by Amazon